# BACKWATER KEY

## A KURT HUNTER MYSTERY

### STEVEN BECKER

THE WHITE MARLIN PRESS

### Get my starter library First Bite for Free! when you sign up for my newsletter

http://eepurl.com/-obDj

First Bite contains the first book in each of Steven Becker's series:

- **Wood's Reef**
- **Pirate**
- **Bonefish Blues**

By joining you will receive one or two emails a month about what I'm doing and special offers.

Your contact information and privacy are important to me. I will not spam or share your email with anyone.

**Wood's Reef**

"A riveting tale of intrigue and terrorism, Key West characters in their *full glory! Fast paced and continually changing direction Mr Becker has me hooked on his skillful and adventurous tales from the Conch Republic!"*

**Pirate**
*"A gripping tale of pirate adventure off the coast of 19th Century Florida!"*

**Bonefish Blues***"I just couldn't put this book down. A great plot filled with action. Steven Becker brings each character to life, allowing the reader to become immersed in the plot."*

**Get them now (http://eepurl.com/-obDj)**

Copyright © 2018 by Steven Becker
All rights reserved.
No part of this book may be reproduced in any form or by any electronic or mechanical means, including information storage and retrieval systems, without written permission from the author, except for the use of brief quotations in a book review.

―――――

Join my mailing list
and get a free copy of Wood's Ledge
http://mactravisbooks.com

# 1

I WAS GOING THE WRONG WAY. THE BIG CLUE WAS WHEN I LOOKED UP and saw a stream of air bubbles flowing toward the surface instead of the diver that had been there a second ago. In an effort to avoid the pink fins kicking at my head, I had pressed the discharge button on my buoyancy compensator and released too much air. It took a few seconds for my training to kick in and my finger moved to the inflator button. A fresh injection of air allowed me to continue my ascent and a minute later I relaxed when I saw the pink fins again.

They belonged to my daughter, Allie, and though I was a novice, with only a handful of dives in my logbook, this was her first open-water experience. She had already aced the pool training and the two protected water dives on her path toward becoming a certified diver. I glanced down for one more look at the spectacular coral formations forty feet below and with a kick of my fins, raised my hand above my head and broke through the surface. I squinted in the brilliant sun looking for Allie, and had a quick moment of panic until I spun in a circle and found her. The smile on her face was one of those memories of raising her that I would never forget.

I looked over at her and, not wanting to endanger her training, raised my right arm, formed a semi-circle, and touched the top of my head with my hand, giving the universal okay sign. She took my cue and did the same before kicking over to the buoy line drifting behind the boat. I followed and a minute later Justine helped us aboard.

TJ gathered up the two other divers also working on their certifications and we were soon stripping off our gear in the shade of the flybridge of his boat.

"That was amazing," Allie said.

Justine came down and joined us. She hadn't done this dive, having scheduled a mixed-air dive with TJ's wife, Alicia later. The ex-CIA analyst and her husband owned and operated *Deep Down Divers* in Key Largo.

"What was your favorite part?" Justine asked.

"We saw a turtle. That was really cool, but it was all great."

The two had become close over the last few weeks since I had been granted some visitation rights with Allie. Justine had been instrumental in the transition and it warmed me to see the two of them together and how well they got along. It was also a little scary how it seemed like the three of us had become a family. Allie had helped move our relationship to level seven on a scale of eight. I was almost ready to take that last step.

"Did you see that school of snapper?" I had never dove Pennekamp Park before. My checkout dives had been closer to the shop. Today, the weather had been near perfect and with a full contingent of six paying customers, TJ had agreed to the extra fuel to run to the park.

"They were really cool the way they moved together. I've seen it in videos, but it was so cool in person."

"I've never seen fish like that."

"It's not like that everywhere?" Allie asked, her smile fading just a bit.

"It's like the fish know the boundaries of the protected area. There're lots of fish outside the park, but this is special. Let's switch over our gear and get ready for the next dive." I didn't want anything to mute her excitement.

"Going to move out a bit deeper to the Hole in the Wall." TJ explained as he climbed down the ladder from the bridge and went forward.

We were tied to one of the mooring balls on Molasses Reef. The engines started and Alicia nosed the bow forward, placing enough slack for TJ to release the line. She idled through the field of scattered white balls, most with boats tied to them. Justine, Allie, and I all leaned over the gunwales and watched the water change from a clear top-to-bottom turquoise to a deeper indigo with a few darker spots only hinting at what lay below. As a special agent in Biscayne National Park, just to the north of Key Largo, I see this water everyday and it still takes my breath away.

The procedure was reversed at the new spot and once TJ had secured the boat, we started to change over our BCs and regulators to fresh tanks.

It was interesting how quickly setting up the gear had become routine, and I watched Allie after I had finished mine. I had started over to help but caught a look from TJ that told me to let her do it herself. As I watched her it amazed me how she had grown and aged more than I had thought possible in the year we had been separated. She was now fifteen, and every bit of a teenager; more grown up than the tween I remembered. Justine had been speculating, based on the amount of time she had her face buried in her phone that she had a boyfriend, but I was in denial—not ready for that step yet.

Daniel J. Viscount, hopefully my ex-attorney, had performed the miracle that he promised only he could provide and gotten me every other weekend and holidays with Allie. At least for now, my ex and I were on good enough terms that hopefully his services would no longer be needed. It wasn't the usual sex or money that had split us up, but rather my work and the angry cartel that had firebombed our house. Separately we had both made the move across country, Jane to her sister's and me to Adams Key.

The move had been what the park service had offered as their witness protection program. After discovering the largest pot grow ever found on public land out in the Plumas National Forest in

Northern California, my family and I had incurred the wrath of the cartel.

The emergency custody hearing had lasted all of five minutes and it had taken a year and all the wiles and experience of Daniel J. Viscount to level the playing field. This was our second full weekend together after the half-dozen visits it had taken to get her this far toward her certification. Again, I had to hand it to Justine for the ingenuity in getting father and daughter together.

After securing the boat to the buoy, TJ came back from the bow and called the four divers over for the dive briefing. We were going to sixty feet this time and he explained the terrain, bottom time, and ascent. On the way up we would practice a ten-minute safety stop. The hour-long surface interval had passed quickly and we were soon back in the water.

I could tell that Allie was more relaxed on this dive. On the first, she had been required to perform several techniques for her certification. This time, with the exception of the safety stop, it was all for fun. I followed happily behind as Allie glided through the coral heads and slots between the reefs. Fish were schooled under every overhang, with barracudas lurking around the corner waiting to pick off an unsuspecting specimen. With TJ leading us we found the large hole that the dive was named for and when he positioned Allie and I for a picture, I thought that Justine should be there too.

We passed the next thirty minutes blissfully blowing bubbles until TJ got our attention and we headed back to the line anchoring the mooring ball. Once we were together, we ascended to ten feet and started the safety stop. I was excited for Allie, knowing in ten minutes she would be a certified diver.

TJ signaled that the time had elapsed and I looked over at Allie. I smiled seeing the look of pure joy on her face. Together we swam under the boat and surfaced at the ladder. Allie's confidence was evident as she removed her fins, placed them in her left hand and climbed aboard unassisted. I envied her youth; the minute my thirty-eight-year-old body left the water, gravity took over and I felt the pains of my years.

"Congratulations," TJ announced to the newly certified divers. They high-fived each other and while TJ and Alicia released the line and moved the boat to deeper water for Justine's dive, we stripped our gear and placed it in our mesh bags which we stashed beneath the bench.

Looking over the side as we crossed the reef, we could see the water become darker—soon the bottom was completely obscured. Justine's dive was scheduled for one-hundred-ten feet, just twenty feet shy of the limit for recreational divers. There were no buoys this deep and I watched TJ and Alicia work together using the GPS and depth finder to locate the dive spot.

"Drop it," Alicia called out.

TJ threw a large orange Styrofoam buoy over the side and I watched the line pay off of it as the weight sank to the bottom. Once it had settled, Alicia moved the boat up-current while TJ went to the bow to release the anchor. When the boat was about a hundred feet from the buoy she called for him to drop it. The anchor splashed into the sea and the chain rattled through the guides. The boat finally settled about ten feet from the buoy.

Justine was getting ready and Allie had disappeared. I found her sitting in the sun on the deck in front of the cabin frantically working her phone. Though I wanted to go up and be with her, I also knew she needed her time alone. As much as it hurt, I sat down by myself.

A few minutes later Justine and Alicia were in the water. Allie was still on the foredeck and the other couple was taking selfies off the starboard side.

"Why don't you bring a couple of beers up," TJ called from the bridge.

I reached into the cooler and grabbed two cans, then a coke that I brought to Allie. I received only a grunt for thanks, but I ignored the teenage mood swing, and took the beer up to the bridge.

"She did really well. A lot of the kids her age have panic attacks. Lot of drama going on in those teen years."

I nodded and opened the beers. Handing one to him, I took a sip of mine. TJ and I had a formed a bond stronger than your basic friendship. Just after I relocated here we had ended up working, together with Mac Travis and Trufante, to bring down a human smuggling ring. When you are under fire with someone, you look at them differently. "She's a good kid."

"How're you going to make out if those idiots in Washington shut down the government?" he asked.

If there had been a black cloud hanging over the day, that was it. The opposing parties in D.C. agreed on little, which was generally okay with me even if they didn't get much done, but their political posturing was now about to affect my paycheck. I didn't have much in terms of expenses, except the alimony and child support I paid to Jane. But with no paycheck and little savings, I knew defaulting on those payments would be something even Daniel J. Viscount would not be able to do anything about, especially since there was no way I could pay him.

"I'll get by. They're talking about keeping us on this time." The last shutdown had closed the National Parks. I wasn't sure how that would work with Biscayne, as it was mostly water. There was no way to put barricades around it.

"Sure hope so. Seen a big uptick in suspicious activity lately. Did you see that piece in the paper about heroin getting popular again?"

Just as he spoke we heard a sound that could only be made by multiple outboards. Both of us instinctively panned the horizon for the source, and a few minutes later we saw the forty-foot-plus, narrow-beamed go-fast boat cruise by. I looked over at the two men at the helm, and then the boat, noticing there were no fishing poles aboard.

"Hey, Dad, did you see that boat? Way cool!" Allie called up from the foredeck.

I looked behind us now and saw the other couple trying to get a selfie with the boat in the background. It was quickly fading over the horizon. I turned back to Allie, trying to think of a nice way to tell her that it wasn't all that cool.

## 2

Back at the dock we said our good-byes and made plans for our next visit in two weeks. It had been a great day until the black cloud of the inevitable government shutdown had blown our way. I tried to put it behind me as I took Allie's picture with her Open Water Certification card. The minute we hit the truck, her head was buried in her phone, posting it on Facebook and Instagram. The speed limit drive back to headquarters surprised me; this might have been the only time I would have preferred some traffic to prolong the day. Justine was heading back to Miami and I had to go back to Adams Key. We had already agreed that she would drive Allie to meet her mom. After hugging them both, I watched Justine's car pull out of the parking lot.

Suddenly I felt out of sorts, and turned to the dock where my boat was tied off in its usual slip next to Susan McLeash's. I jumped aboard my twenty-two-foot center-console park service boat and started the engine. After untying the bowlines I went to the stern, surprised to see that one of Susan's lines was over mine. I glanced over at her boat and saw footprints in the green dusting of pollen. It surprised me that the boat appeared to have been recently used. My sometimes partner and often nemesis had been reassigned to guiding tours pending a review of some of her actions. As I understood it, the boat was supposedly off limits.

Filing away the incident in my memory, I decided to temporarily let her off the hook. She had caught me icing down some snapper across the way at Bayfront Park a few weeks ago, and I was still surprised she hadn't shown the pictures to our boss, at least not yet. Hopefully now I had something on her. I put it from my mind as I pulled into the channel, where I had to concentrate on the long line of boats coming toward the public ramp. After a day on the water, some boaters were quiet; others loud and partying. It was spring break season, which always added to the usual traffic of a beautiful Sunday on the water. If I had been on duty, several boats might have been of interest. I let that thought go when I saw the Florida Fish and Wildlife Commission boat off to the side, randomly pulling boaters over to check their licenses and catch. I nodded to the officers as I passed, thinking to myself that they'd chosen a pretty lazy way to police the waters.

Before I could start an internal rant about the FWC, my phone vibrated and I picked it up. There was a text from Allie thanking me for everything. Instead of a "love you", there was a big heart emoji at the end. I texted back the old school "love you too" and smiled to myself. Life was good.

Even the impending shutdown wasn't going to ruin my day. Maybe it should have, but I didn't think it would matter. Guessing at unintended consequences had been my undoing before, but I couldn't see how the looming shutdown would affect me. The furlough orders had come through, but I didn't believe they actually intended to shut down the park. Ninety percent of the park's 275 square miles was water. Between the string of barrier islands and the shoreline on the mainland, there were hundreds of miles, and many smugglers' havens.

The last go 'round, the government had made a show of blockading off park entrances. That wasn't going to work here. The boat ramps were operated by either the cities or Dade County who charged for their use. I expected they'd be unaffected by the political machinations in Washington, but this news had put my boss, Martinez, at his breaking point for the last few weeks. He was a doom-and-gloom kind of guy, who thought he controlled the park from the three computer monitors sitting on his desk. If the government shutdown and the screens went dark, in his mind, so would the park. It was, as always, his budget he was concerned with, and he knew another sequester was likely and the park's funding would be automatically reduced. To a desk jockey who rode those numbers day in and day out, that could be devastating.

My official capacity as special agent in the park would be on hold, but my park service house out on Adams Key, my park service boat, and my truck were safe—at least for the short term. I would still be out on the water every day, and if problems arose, I would take care of them, shutdown or not. The worst that could happen was that my park service credit card would be refused and I would have to buy my own gas.

Some employees felt differently. Susan McLeash, for one, was bitter and vowed to stay home and ride out the shutdown in front of her makeup mirror. Without a paycheck, she might have to pick and choose her happy hours. Martinez would be forced to downgrade his golf game and play the public courses. He had called a staff meeting for the next morning, to tell us all his master plan if the apocalyptic scenario occurred. It wouldn't be his best moment; those were reserved for the podium.

The boat was up on plane now, skipping over the small waves as I passed the last marker for the shared channel leading from Bayfront Park and the headquarters building to the open bay. I accelerated, vowing that the smile on my face was not going away, no matter what happened. It was all good, I thought, as I cruised across the pristine flats of the bay. Winter was a memory and the cold fronts were fewer and less severe, allowing for weeks of beautiful weather between them. We were in one of these periods now.

Several boats racing toward me brought my focus back to the water. I looked around the bay, seeing almost twice as much traffic as I'd have expected. During the week, the park was generally quiet, but on weekends, the massive parking lots of Black Point and Bayfront Parks were filled to capacity. This was prime time—past the winter winds but before the summer heat and daily thunderstorms. It almost looked like some of the ski lakes in Northern California.

I dodged several more boats and stayed wide of the direct route to Adams Key and Caesar Creek. Having creek in the name was a misnomer for the channel running between the bay and the Atlantic. Tides and currents affected the well-traveled inlet, making it tricky to navigate. Being the closest to the two major boat ramps, it was a high-traffic area, and I wanted nothing to do with the boatloads full of coeds and partiers heading back to the mainland.

It was when I made the turn back to Adams Key, which lay on the bay side of Caesar Creek, that I saw the crab boat running north. The park was off-limits to traps, and this was a strange enough sight that I took notice. There was no good reason and more than a few bad ones for the boat to be transiting the bay. Dark smoke poured from the exhaust on the transom of the boat, telling me she was running near or at her top speed. I changed my heading to run parallel to the boat, but stayed far enough away so as to not cause them to change course.

Following a boat on the water is different from following a vehicle. Except for the area adjacent to the few marked channels, the entire bay was navigable. Unless both boats are clearly headed for the same point, such as an inlet or marina, there is no reason to follow someone. It's better to stay as far back as possible and still keep the boat in sight. This was my plan as I headed back to the center of the bay, allowing the crab boat the shoreline. We passed the long concrete dock at Adams Key and I thought about just going home, but a crab boat running the bay late on a Sunday afternoon was uncommon.

I just wasn't sure it was unusual enough to pursue. First, it was my day off, and second, I still had that smile on my face from a nearly perfect day. But there is something in my DNA that takes some of these decisions out of my control. I passed my home on Adams Key and started up the miles-long mangrove-covered coast of Elliot Key, making a deal with myself that if the boat continued past Stiltsville, the water-bound group of buildings at the northern end of the park that I would turn back. The structures now reduced to seven after the last hurricane, were one of the few things that Martinez and I both agreed on. They were bad for his budget and a refuge for nefarious activity.

The crab boat and I were forced closer together about halfway up Elliot Key. Toward its northern end was a long no-motor zone, and to the west lay the Featherbed Banks, a large shoal ridden area that was best avoided. Because of the natural funnel, I backed off on the throttle, allowing the crabber to slip ahead. Without a light bar, and with the park service insignia below the bow flare, I doubted they had even noticed the nondescript boat. The green fabric on the T-top was the only identifying feature, and would be invisible from this distance.

The crabber continued unabated, blowing its wake into the mangroves. Sands Key lay just ahead and Boca Chita, the last and most northern key in the miles long chain of barrier islands, lay on the other side of Lewis Cut. He increased speed, and my smile faded when I saw the silt trail behind the boat as its propeller scarred the bottom of the turtle grass-covered bottom. This was a delicate ecosystem, which supported fish and crabs; one that took years to replace.

Even though my boat didn't draw as much water as the larger, heavier crabber, I hit the small button on the throttle to raise the tilt of the engine and followed. The trail darkened as the Crabber's propeller tore through the bottom. I didn't need to worry about keeping the boat in sight with the stream of muck trailing behind it.

Finally, they reached Sands Cut and found the deep-water channel. I was about to turn back when they turned into the pass, but then I wondered what reason they had for staying inside the barrier islands at all and risking the ire of the rangers and FWC officers for tearing up the seagrass bottom. I was still short of Boca Chita Key and decided to keep following them. The worst that would happen was that I would take the outside route back home.

Entering Sands Cut I accelerated to offset the effect of the current and saw the crabber ahead turn north after the last marker. When he stopped and dropped anchor just offshore of Boca Chita, I knew something was wrong.

Boca Chita Key, with its iconic lighthouse and campground, was generally well-visited, and today was no different. The small island also had the advantage of a protected harbor and an actual beach, something rare for the park. A park service boat cruising these waters would be a normal sight, and nothing to alarm the crabber. That gave me the confidence to move closer. They were technically doing nothing wrong, except whatever had brought them to these waters was still a mystery to me.

The only thing that might look out of place with a close pass was that I was out of uniform, and that was something that would put a suspicious captain on guard. Taking the chance that they were here for a reason, I decided to use my shorts and T-shirt to my advantage and have a look from land. Staying to the deeper water, I worked north around the point of the small island and with the lighthouse on my port side, turned into the harbor.

A long concrete seawall encased the cove and I had to take a minute to drop my fenders before approaching. I slid into a space between several larger boats, tied off the boat, and hopped onto the path running alongside the harbor. The beach where I could observe the crabber was directly across the island, and I took off at a fast walk through the mostly full campground. The spring and fall were the best seasons to camp here; the heat was tolerable, and the mosquito count lower than during the summer months.

Trying to avoid invading on occupied sites, I serpentined my way to the beach and looked out over the calm Atlantic. The crabber was anchored in about ten feet of water, less than a hundred yards off the beach. There were at least eight men aboard; more than would normally crew a boat of this size, and they didn't look like fishermen. I pulled out my camera and with the zoom on its maximum setting, took several pictures, hoping the computer screen would reveal the origin of the tattoo that seemed common to each man.

## 3

BESIDES THE SIMILAR TATTOOS, THERE WAS SOMETHING ABOUT THEM that said gang. Maybe it was the uniform look and dress, or the camaraderie. They weren't wearing colors—mostly black tank tops and jeans, which still looked out of place here—but there was enough ink on the men to have furnished several tattoo shop owners a healthy retirement.

I stayed and watched as the shadows grew longer, and the men became drunker and louder. Empty bottles were tossed in the water and a fight broke out near the stern. After that things settled down for a few minutes—before I heard the first shotgun fire. Several more blasts followed and I was surprised to see flames and sparks shooting form the muzzles of the some of the guns. Fortunately they were shooting toward the open water and not the island, so no one in the gathering crowd was in danger.

Then something went in the water, followed by two men who dove in to retrieve it. The display of firepower ended and the weight of the men as they leaned over the gunwale watching was enough for the boat to list heavily toward that side. The crabber was built to carry stacks of heavy crab traps and I had no fear that it would sink. Just as the sun set the two men climbed back aboard empty-handed.

The sounds of the argument that followed was obscured when the engine started with a belch of black smoke. I watched as they pulled anchor and headed back toward Sand Key. I called the disturbance in to Miami-Dade in case they continued and I needed backup, and decided to shadow them. Only a foolish man would try to board a boat full of drunken gangbangers, especially alone, and I doubted Miami-Dade would reach the area before the crew disappeared into one of the myriad creeks and channels in the southern part of the park. I wasn't surprised when the dispatcher said they would be standing by in case there was trouble, but they had no interest in a reconnaissance trip. Our jurisdictions were separated by dotted lines on a map and our cases often overlapped. That didn't mean either agency liked that.

As I followed them past Adams Key, I tried to theorize why they had been there. Ignoring coincidences was bad for business—and the government shutdown, still scheduled for midnight—and what looked like a show of strength from a gang was definitely not something to be ignored. I followed until the boat turned into the channel and headed out Caesar Creek. After the crabber slowly moved offshore and to the south, I decided they weren't my problem anymore—at least not today

Just as I reached the dock, my neighbors Becky and Ray's pit bull mix Zero came barreling down the concrete walkway. His toenails skidded to a stop by the bow and he looked at me, and then the rest of the boat. Giving a short bark to express his dissatisfaction that I was alone, he backed away and collapsed onto the warm dock. I called out to him and his stubby tail wagged, but I could tell he was disappointed. I hardly ignored him, but Allie and Justine paid him the attention he believed he was entitled to.

"Where's your girls at?" Becky asked as she came toward the boat.

"Allie has school tomorrow and Justine drove her to meet her mom."

"If I was you, I'd be watching that business of them women together. Careful there," she said.

Becky and Ray, along with their three-year-old, Jamie, and Zero lived in the other house on Adams Key. With its large well-manicured clearing, the small island was unusual for this area. It was a rare to find open land on these mosquito-infested, mangrove-covered islands. Adams and some of the adjacent keys were labeled on some charts as Islandia. It was a romantic-sounding name for a swamp that had been given to the area by a group of developers in the 1920s. Originally called Cocolobo Key, what is now Adams once hosted the Cocolobo Cay Club, a famous resort that claimed to have hosted four presidents. After the club fell into decay, the eye of hurricane Andrew finished off whatever was left of it and its surrounding buildings. All that remained now was the clearing, with our two park service houses and a small day use area accessed by the long concrete dock.

You didn't have to look very hard to see signs on most of the barrier islands showing different developers' attempts over the years to carve out a slice of paradise. Deep-water, dead-end canals were common signs left over from the period before the government had put a stop to dredging. Over time, most of the land-based attempts to tame the islands had been retaken by nature.

"What's Ray going to do about the shutdown?" I asked. My neighbor Ray maintained Adams Key as well as the campgrounds and facilities on the other out islands. He had the unique ability to fight off the salt, sun, bugs, and brush to keep everything working on the islands, but he was a rough guy, the kind that the bureaucrats had a hard time living with. But even Martinez, for all his complaining, knew that it would be harder to live without him than with him.

"Fish a bit more, but I know the old coot. He won't let his territory fall too far."

"Yeah, Martinez has called a staff meeting for tomorrow morning." I figured I should tell her because Ray was likely to blow it off.

"Y'all should go just to watch him squirm," she laughed. "I would if I could."

"Tell Ray I'll ride over with him. Probably ought to hoard some of the government gas before we have to start buying our own."

"Right about that. Y'all want to watch the dog for a bit. Jamie's been sick and I could use some sleep."

"Sure thing. Tell Ray I'm leaving at eight." This was pretty much standard procedure at least twice a week. When Justine stayed over, she would volunteer, but I always accepted the company. Zero could be a pain, though. He was the island's alarm, notifying the occupants whenever a boat was near the dock. My house was set back farther than Ray and Becky's, making it less of an issue for me, but even though the dock was clearly marked as a Day Use Area, we still had some nighttime visitors.

I called for the dog to follow and after hosing down the boat, started toward my house. The euphoria I had felt earlier had been replaced by dread at what the shutdown would do to the park. I had been through this once already, out west in 2013 when we had lost funding for almost two weeks. There was some good that might come out of it. Without Martinez dictating my schedule or Susan McLeash waiting in ambush for me to misstep, there would be no patrol schedule and I could pick my fishing spots.

I had learned that fishing was a great way to do my job, though it often landed me in trouble. Back in the Plumas Forest, I had been fly fishing one of the streams when I noticed a current running the wrong way through an eddy. Without a rod in my hand, I never would have found the irrigation inlet that led me to uncover the pot grow that had changed my life. Here in Biscayne, I had already found a handful of bodies while fishing the backwaters.

Those events would not deter me. When I had a fishing rod in hand, I felt at one with my surroundings, and noticed things I would not normally see. Chico, one of the local guides that I had befriended, gave me pointers on some of the out of the way spots that had paid off both in fish and trouble. "Out of the way" was a misnomer here—the miles of mangrove shoreline and winding channels, some manmade but most natural, gave people not wanting to be found the perfect opportunity. And all in sight of the Miami skyline.

What had been a perfect day ended in an uneasy night. Rather than reliving the memories of diving with Allie, the crab boat was on my mind. With the exception of the cartel, we hadn't had much in the way of gangs in the Plumas Forest. Motorcycle clubs were more common and the nearby foothill towns were often overrun with rides. Most were clubs out for a day of riding; others were up to no good.

Unable to sleep, I got up early. After turning on the coffee pot, I opened my laptop and downloaded the pictures I had taken yesterday. Despite maxing out the zoom, several were clear enough to make out the tattoos. Google took less than two seconds to identify the men as Outlaws. California was still Hells Angels territory; the rest of the country belonged to the Outlaws. On a hunch, I scanned the faces against the FBI's ten most wanted list, and shut down the computer knowing at least none of the men I had seen were on it.

Tendrils of daylight filtering in through the blinds told me the time, and with two hours until Martinez's meeting I needed something to do. Justine was an accomplished standup paddleboard racer, and after trying to keep up with her in a kayak I had found on the island, I had finally bought a board of my own. After changing into board shorts and a dryfit top, I grabbed the board and paddle from the side of the house and carried them to the dock. It was low tide, making the drop to the water close to five feet, but I had devised a system for launching the board. With a dock line attached to the leash plug, I slid the board off the dock and, using the line, brought it to the ladder.

Caesar Creek is known for its strong current and this was the case this morning. With the tide flooding in the pass, I had to drop to my knees and steer directly into it in order to cross the channel and reach the protection of the islands across the way. From there the water flattened out as the current dissipated into the large bay and I was able to stand. For an hour, I worked my way through the small islands that surrounded Jones Lagoon. I was feeling pretty confident and exited on the ocean side in order to ride the current back to Adams Key. On my first attempt, I blew past the dock, but was able to back-paddle and grab the last piling. Zero, of course, not recognizing me on the board, hovered overhead, barking at me.

After a shower and breakfast, I met Ray on the dock and we

headed to the boat. "You still ride?" I asked, remembering something he had said about missing motorcycles out here.

"Used to back home. Been boat bound for a while now and that prick of a boss won't let me store one at headquarters."

"Know anything about the gangs here?"

"The Outlaws are always making the news for one thing or another, but I ain't looking for trouble."

"I hear you," I said, and released the lines to Ray's boat. I was still a novice in his eyes and he preferred to drive. I was a quiet guy, but Ray made me look like a talker, and it was easy for both of us to settle into the rhythm of the seas as the boat cruised west. The crabber and bikers were soon forgotten and I thought of better things: Allie and Justine—until I saw the black smoke on the horizon.

"What do you figure that is?" I leaned into Ray so he could hear me and pointed to the streaming smoke to the north.

"Ain't no wind. Looks to be from Boca Chita."

The chimneys across the water at the Turkey Point Power Plant confirmed this as the smoke gently wafted from them. If there were any breeze they were a sure indicator of its strength and direction.

"Might want to check it out. Could be a fire," I said.

"Hell yeah. Any excuse not to have to listen to that sorry ass boss is good with me," he said, cutting the wheel to port. He drove harder and faster than I dared and a few minutes later, the lighthouse soon came into view and we slowed. He made a wide turn to hit the channel leading to the harbor.

The black cloud was dissipating quickly and I thought we might have wasted the trip as well as the soon-to-be-precious fuel when suddenly, a loud roar came from the harbor. I grabbed the stainless steel support for the T-top as a banana yellow go-fast boat sped from the harbor.

## 4

There was nothing we could do but watch the wake dissipate as the go-fast boat blew through the no-wake zone. Our park service bay boats were practical craft for these waters, but no match for twin three-hundred-horsepower engines. I grabbed the helm for support as the wake passed underneath the boat, throwing me off-balance and making it impossible to focus the binoculars. I strained for a glimpse of the men at the helm. Wearing cut-off denim jackets and skull caps, the two men disappeared from view before I could make out any other distinguishing features. The banana yellow hull stuck out but was not unusual enough in itself to locate the boat later; there were probably hundreds like it in the surrounding marinas.

I had gangs on my mind as we entered the harbor. The ink, cut-off denim, and general disobedience pointed me in that direction. Maybe I was thinking the worst, but coincidences were starting to pile up. Between the timing of the government shutdown, the men aboard the crabber yesterday, and the go-fast boat now, it was hard to believe this was just tourist activity. Then there was the belch of black smoke that had brought us here.

The park was tourist-oriented: boating, fishing, snorkeling, and kayaking were among the popular and legal pastimes. But this was

South Florida and smuggling was always not far from people's minds. Since the '70s, pot and coke had been a major revenue generator in the area. Some speculated that if drugs were a legal commodity, they would dwarf all other imports. With the heavily laden container ships and cruise liners running in and out of Government Cut, that was saying a lot. Generally the smugglers stayed to the southern part of the park, where it morphed into the Keys. That area was littered with mangrove-covered islands and creeks; perfect for clandestine meets.

The fire that had attracted our attention was short-lived, but we were close and decided to check it out anyway. Often on weekends and holidays, the marina resembled a parking lot with boats rafted together against the packed seawall, but today it was quiet, with only a half-dozen boats tied up to the concrete seawall. Then a high-pitched scream broke the silence.

Ray gave me a look when I reached into the watertight compartment below the helm. Our boats were identical and I had instinctively reached for my gun belt, but this was his boat, and it was not there. Wearing the belt is awkward on a boat. The holster is always in the way and no matter how well-oiled I keep it, the harsh saltwater environment attacks the steel. I would put it on when approaching another craft or land, but on the water you can usually see the threat coming. The woman screamed again, and I saw a crowd gathering around the lighthouse.

"Over there." I pointed to an empty spot on the seawall. "Can you drop me?"

Ray nodded and nosed the bow toward the concrete abutment. When the gap closed to six inches I jumped and Ray simultaneously put the engine in reverse and backed away. The minute my feet landed on solid ground, I took off at a run. It was less than fifty yards to the lighthouse. I reached it quickly and I pushed my way past the group gathered in a semi-circle around the entrance. Something dripped from above, and when I looked down at the pool of blood on the ground, I knew it was bad.

I looked up to find its source. It wasn't hard. Hanging over the cast-iron railing of the sixty-five-foot high observation deck was a body. Blood was dripping from a gash across the man's neck. The coincidences I had just been wrestling with had turned into reality. Only eight hours since the government shutdown, the park appeared to be a pawn in some kind of gang-related chess game. Pulling my phone from my pocket, I ushered the crowd into the shade of one of the few nearby palm trees and asked them to wait there until I could take their statements.

There was clearly no need for first responders and nothing to be done about the body until the medical examiner arrived. After pressing the contact button for Martinez, I walked over to the entrance, and with my fingertip pushed the lighthouse door closed to seal the crime scene. The call went to voicemail and I hesitated before leaving a message. I figured he'd stop in the clubhouse for a drink after the ninth hole and get it then. Shutdown or not, and with or without his blessing, I had a case.

My next call was to the Miami-Dade medical examiner's office. The park service had little in the way of infrastructure, and relied on the jurisdiction within which the park lay for services. This often caused friction and I had accumulated more enemies in the ego-bloated halls of Miami-Dade than I would have liked. But there were a few people there that I had cultivated a working relationship with and one was detective Grace Herrera. She was my next call.

While I waited for the medical examiner, I pecked out a quick text to Justine. There was nothing she liked better than a dead body, and I wished it were later in the day. She worked the swing shift for the forensics lab and wouldn't be in until two. After pressing send, I walked over to the shady area and started to interview the witnesses. Most had either been attracted by the smoke or the woman's scream and seen nothing. Even if they had, they'd realized there were probably gangs involved and had erased the incident from their memories. One man, though refusing to give his name, had seen the boat leave. The description he gave was a dead end. The men had worn long sleeves and hoodies over their vests when he'd seen them, clearly hiding their affiliation.

My next call was to Johnny Wells from ICE. His unit was under the jurisdiction of the Department of Justice and not subject to the whims of the politicians on Capitol Hill. After a quick description of the boat and its occupants, he agreed to see if he could locate them. I had ridden along with him and his team on several cases, and had total confidence in their ability. If the go-fast boat was still on the water, they would find it. The problem was, the geographic area was huge. They could have headed south and holed up in a mangrove-covered key, or just as easily gone north and stashed the boat along the industrial section of the Miami River. Those were only two of the likely options open to them. There were many more.

I had just finished taking names and statements when the Miami-Dade police boat pulled up and docked. Vance Able, the head coroner, hopped out of the Contender and strutted over to me. It wasn't a cocky strut, just what I'd called a hipster walk; all the coffee they drank must have added a bounce to their step. Sid, the night shift examiner, would have been my first choice, but I got along well enough with Vance though I'd probably have to dodge his request to take him bonefishing again.

"Are the bones running?" he asked, shaking my hand. The product in his well-groomed hair, beard, and the tips of his mustache glistened in the sun and I could see the mandatory plaid shirt under his scrubs.

"I ran into one of the guides last week, and he said they were starting to bite. Maybe later this week, if you want to try." I offered the carrot, hoping to gain a few points. I really had no problem taking him out; it was more his misplaced expectations of my guiding ability I was worried about. His desire to start with the elusive bonefish rather than working his way up the food chain made for sure disappointment. Add to that his desire to catch one on a fly, and I was totally out of my element. I did okay on my own, mostly on tips from Ray and Chico, but wasn't sure I was up to taking Vance. I had started fishing the park on my patrols, more to learn the ins and outs of the miles of coastline surrounding the park. I'd caught a few fish, and found a few bodies in the process.

We entered the lighthouse and waited a few seconds for our eyes to adjust to the dim light. When we could see, I followed Vance and the deputy that had brought him out up the winding concrete stairs of the block tower. We reached the observation deck and went outside to the narrow catwalk surrounding the lighthouse. I forgot the reason we were here for a second as I stared at the beauty laid out below me. The colors of the water were indescribable, and from this height, the changes in bottom, from seagrass to sand to coral, were clearly visible. Vance brought me back to the present.

He was leaning over the body. "No doubt it's a homicide. We better wait for the crime scene techs." He pulled his oversize phone from his pocket and called for assistance.

I looked around and saw something smoldering and a large black spot where the concrete deck and wall nearby had been scarred by the fire. I walked over to the source of the smoke we had seen. Whoever had committed the murder had burned the victim's colors. It looked like they'd used a ton of accelerant, the likely cause of the smoke we had seen. I kicked at the pile in the center of the burn and saw a sleeveless denim jacket. It was more intact than I had expected. I guess the accelerant had burned itself out before the jacket incinerated.

The body was Vance's concern for now, and realizing it would take an hour before the techs reached the island there were some things I wanted to have a look at. We were done up here for now and walked back down the stairs. "I saw a crabber on the ocean side yesterday and was going to check it out if you want to take a ride while we wait."

"Cool," Vance said.

The deputy stationed himself at the door to the lighthouse. Vance and I walked over to the park service boat.

"Guessin y'all found a body," Ray said.

"Mind if we have a run around the island? I'd like to see the spot the crabber anchored and there's a grass flat nearby I think might interest Vance." I hadn't forgotten the package that I'd seen go overboard either.

He must have caught my meaning and took a hard look at Vance and shook his head. "Ain't nothin' to eat on them flats, but if y'all want to have a look, I'm game."

Vance and I hopped down from the dock and Ray started the boat. After tossing the lines, we idled out of the marina. "They'll call when the crime techs get here?" I asked.

"Can't do anything without me," he said, grinning like a little boy.

I nodded to Ray and he pushed down on the throttle. The boat jumped up on plane harder and faster than I would have dared. We turned to the south and Ray navigated through the markers for Lewis Cut. I pointed to where I had seen the crabber and as we approached, he raised the engine out of the water and dropped to an idle. Fortunately the water was clear and we could see the line between the deeper sand and the shallow flat. There were plenty of prop scars cut through the brown bottom, but one was fresh.

There were few differences between our boats, but Ray's lacked a Power-Pole, so we were forced to position the boat and anchor alongside the new scar. Ray set us right next to it, and I peered into the crystal clear water. Turtle grass waved in the current and I saw a few of the discarded beer bottles that had been tossed overboard by the gang on the crabber.

"There're fish here," Vance said, pointing to a school actively feeding nearby.

I could tell he was excited and wondered if the whole fly fishing thing was a little over his head. Ray caught it, too, and looked over to me. I nodded and he reached into the console, bringing out a spinning rod with an artificial lure made to look like a shrimp.

"Want to give it a shot?" I asked.

"Heck yeah. Just tell me what to do."

I handed him the rod, and realized he was a total novice. After showing him how to work the bail and drag, I explained how to twitch the rod to make the shrimp appear alive. It turned out he didn't need the last bit of information. On his first cast, he reeled in a small mackerel. He looked to Ray, who took the fish by the gills, removed the hook, and tossed him in the forward cooler. Vance was clearly enjoying himself and the bonefish talk was gone as he reeled in several more fish. After half a dozen, he was experienced with the drag and when the rod bent deeply, he tightened it slightly and started to pump the rod up and down, reeling in line on the downstroke.

"Ain't no fish fights like that," Ray said after watching him struggle for a few minutes. "Watch that line. She snags, she's gonna break."

He was right, and I watched as Ray went to Vance and instructed him to tighten the drag. Without the pull of a live fish, the line came in slowly, and a minute later we were all leaning over the side looking at a black duffel bag.

## 5

I leaned over the side and helped Ray pull the package to the boat. Vance continued to reel the slack line until the duffel was alongside, where Ray used the boathook and tried to lift it from the water. Made for retrieving lines, the lightweight aluminum shaft was no match for the water-logged bag.

"Kurt, can you give a hand here?" Ray asked.

I reached over to help and together we hauled it over the gunwale. The three of us gathered around and stared at the water draining out of it. I estimated it weighed close to fifty pounds.

"When I was watching the crabber yesterday, I saw something go overboard. They searched for it, but it got dark before they found it." It had to be the bag. There was only a light green slime built up on it. It couldn't have been in the water long.

"Can you mark the spot on your GPS? I might need to come back and take a look." I had only seen one bag go over, but I could have missed something.

"We going to look?" Vance asked.

He looked more excited about finding the bag than about the fish he had caught. I thought for a minute, trying to decide if opening it would destroy any evidence. When a crab crawled through a small crack in the zipper, I figured there'd be no harm. The sea had already erased any forensics.

"Sure. You caught it, take the honors."

Vance moved carefully to the bag, moving around it as if it was alive. Finally, standing back as if it could be a bomb, he extended one hand and with two fingers and pulled the zipper open. A large package lay in the shadows of the bag. I moved closer and opened the bag wider. It was clear now that we had found. They called them square grouper; waterproofed packages of drugs thrown from boats or planes when the authorities were closing in. This hadn't been intended for the water, but was still encased in clear plastic. Despite the heavy wrapping a small amount of water had seeped into the white powder packed inside.

"Holy crap," Vance said, moving closer to inspect the package. "Is that what I think it is?"

"Yup." I didn't share his excitement. Finding drugs had wrecked my life and torn apart my family when I'd found the pot grow out west, and now a fifty-pound package of what I guessed was cocaine or heroin lay at my feet. After our history with the cartel and after just normalizing relations with my ex and daughter, this might as well have been a bomb.

I turned my focus to the business at hand. Vance had his camera out and was taking pictures of the package. I stopped him, thinking about Martinez's ability to use the Cloud to pull all the data from my life up on the triple screens in his office. I had no idea where these pictures might end up and wanted this to remain under wraps for a while, not be on the News at Six, or Facebook. He put the phone away, and I looked back at Ray. "The numbers?"

"Go on," he said. I went to the helm, hit the MAN OVERBOARD button, and took a picture of the display. Martinez might see it, but he wouldn't know what it represented. Easing the boat into gear, I moved up on the anchor while Ray pulled in the line. It was full of muck when it cleared the water, and he shook and dunked it several times to clean it off before bringing it aboard. Once it was stowed, he came back to the helm and I stepped to the side. Cutting the wheel, he accelerated before the wind could push us farther onto the flat and I watched him as he steered us into deeper water. He never once looked at the depth finder; instead, he used the color of the water ahead of us as a depth gauge, and I remembered one of the first boating lessons he had given me: brown, brown, run aground.

There was still no sign of the crime scene techs when we reached the marina and I looked at my watch, thinking *They should have been here by now*. We tied off, leaving a space for the CSI crew, and I watched Vance pace the dock. He made a call and came back to the boat. I had remained aboard to keep an eye on the package lying on the deck. Ray had gone to the lighthouse more worried about the blood-stained concrete, than the body or the package.

"They had to bring someone in," Vance said. "Should be out anytime."

My heart leapt thinking it was going to be Justine, but I was conflicted. As much as I wanted to see her, I wanted no one I knew or liked around this. Gangs were all about retribution and knew few boundaries. My concerns were put aside when I saw her smile as soon as the boat pulled into the harbor. I counted five aboard: the deputy at the helm and Justine were behind console, with two techs I had seen around the lab sitting by the transom. A man who looked like a gorilla wearing a business suit stood off to the side. There was no doubt in my mind he was FBI. They docked and business suit was first onto the seawall.

"Agent Hunter?" The man asked. "I'm Ron Pierce, FBI."

I was surprised when I shook his hand and it was warm; his mouth turned up in a half smile that seemed authentic. But his body language clearly said that he thought he was above the rest of us. I looked him in the eye before releasing his hand and saw something that could be described as life in his eyes—not your stereotypical robotic agent. It seemed unusual that he was here—at least so quickly—and I tried to figure out who had said the word *gang*.

The Hells Angels are a club. The Outlaws are a club. Many

motorcycle riders belong to clubs. There are also chess clubs, garden clubs, book clubs, and boxing clubs. The line where they become gangs is blurry. Often, without the majority of the members' knowledge or approval, the club will cross a line, and once they do there is no going back. Petty stuff stays at the state and location level, but when it becomes systemic the Feds will label it ongoing criminal activity and get involved, using the RICO Act in an attempt to disband the organization. I recalled the tattoos from the crabber and the man hanging from the balcony. The Outlaws definitely fell into the latter class.

Justine smiled at me and I caught a quick wink. She was probably so excited by the dead body that the FBI agent's presence hadn't raised a red flag with her. I took her case as she stepped up to the dock, but knew better than to offer a hand. The two other techs handed up their cases and we walked over to the lighthouse.

We stood staring at the body in silence.

"Y'all gonna get that down before it stains the concrete any worse?" Ray called out.

That brought me back to reality, and I realized the silence was from lack of authority, not out of respect for the deceased. "Let's split up and get these scenes processed."

"Plural?" Justine asked.

"We found a square grouper in the water. It's on the boat."

"Body first," she said, leading the other two techs into the lighthouse.

"I'd like to have a look at what you have aboard," Pierce said.

Ray followed us to the boat. Like mine, this was his personal vessel as well. I had fishing poles aboard; there was no telling what he had.

"Found it around the back of the island," I said as we hopped down to the deck. I wasn't ready to tell him about following the crab boat yesterday.

He carefully opened the duffel bag and reached inside. Removing the package, he gently laid it on the deck. "Mind?" he asked, pulling a pocketknife from his pocket and opening the blade.

"Guess there's not much for forensics after being in the water." I wanted to say the words for the record.

"You're probably right there." He opened the blade, inserted it into the package, and made a two-inch slit. Removing the knife, he touched the tip to his tongue. "Heroin."

"Let me get one of the techs and we'll bag and tag it." I hopped onto the dock, leaving Ray and Ron staring at each other. I was glad that Ray remained with the FBI agent. He wouldn't try anything with Ray watching.

Walking back to the lighthouse, I thought about what had happened. It seemed pretty straightforward. The lost package was supposed to have been placed on the island for a pickup this morning. It wasn't there, and when the meet took place, the buyer must have taken out the rival gang member assigned to collect the money. Business was business, and there was no trust among these groups.

I looked up at the lighthouse, noticing that the body had been removed from the rail. I walked around the blood pool on the concrete walkway, now ringed with crime scene tape, and heard voices echoing off the concrete block walls when I entered.

"Agent, can you give us a hand here?" Vance called from the steps.

They were trying to haul the body bag down the circular stairs. The six-foot-long corpse was already stiff and not cooperating. There was no way to do this as a group. I moved to the body, grasped one end, and motioned to one of the deputies to get the other end. Together we did the best we could to move it down the stairs without causing any further damage. The victim was a heavy man and I barely made it out the door at the bottom before my legs caved in and I dumped my end of the bag on the ground. The deputy and I stood on either end, bent over at the waist for several minutes with our hands on our hips, struggling to catch our breath.

"Nice, Hercules. Wonder if the government will still be paying your insurance while they're closed?" Justine asked.

She said it with sass, but it was actually a good question. "Wait 'til you see what's on the boat." I started walking to the dock. She was at my side in seconds. There wasn't much she liked better than a dead body, but the unknown hooked her. "Anything up there?"

"Body, blood, concrete. DNA and concrete don't get along. Might be something under the vic's fingernails if he fought, but that's probably all we're going to get."

"He's definitely gang."

"Yup."

We reached the dock and I was about to hop down to the deck of the boat when I heard the sound of a twin engine outboard. The Miami-Dade Contender entered the marina but it slowed too late and its wake slammed against the boats tied to the concrete seawall. I had been forced to ride with the captain and crew before and didn't like them, but when the man standing behind the leaning post turned, I liked him less. On the front deck was Grace Herrera with a line in her hand. She was the only chance I had of making this civil.

"Oh great, Ranger Rick and the Feds," Grace's partner called out.

He, along with several of his buddies, had taken to using the nickname Justine had given me. There was no question it held a different meaning for them. I bit my tongue and waited for Grace.

"I just got the call, guess the Feds beat me to it when they heard the victim was inked up."

I shrugged, not understanding who had what to say about anything here. To make matters worse, Martinez had not called back. He was apparently taking the furlough seriously. I was on my own. "Vance has the body ready to go back." I thought just stating the facts would pacify them.

"You got no jurisdiction here, Pierce," Dick Tracy said, turning from me to the Fed.

Grace's partner and I were hardly on good terms. I didn't know if he was protective of her or maybe jealous. Having been given the name of the cartoon detective probably didn't help either—he didn't need a nickname.

Pierce stayed above the fray and looked away, but Tracy remained undeterred and walked toward the boat. I saw Ron try and push the duffel out of sight with his foot, but Tracy had seen it as well.

"What'cha got there, Mr. Fed?"

He didn't wait for an answer and climbed down to the deck.

"This is a federal matter. RICO Act takes precedence," Pierce said.

"Right, when it's convenient. I get it. If you're on a case, you're not furloughed." Tracy moved to the duffel and kicked it to the side. "Grace," he called out. "It's Christmas."

## 6

Government shutdown day one, and already we had a dead body, a pile of heroin, and two turf wars about to break out. The one between Miami-Dade and the FBI would be resolved by some bureaucrat. The gang war would likely only be resolved with more blood. Dick Tracy and Ron Pierce had already squared off and were ready for a fight as we stared at the package on the deck of the boat.

"All of you off," Justine called down. "I don't care who has jurisdiction; I want a look at it before y'all bugger up the evidence."

The two men looked at my girl standing on the dock with her hands on her hips. They glanced at each other, and the only thing left to resolve was who would disembark first. Ron proved to be the bigger man, and also the closest. Tracy followed him.

"You, too, Special Agent," Justine said, as she lowered herself to the deck and reached behind her for her case.

The three of us stood on the dock watching Justine as she worked. It was hard not to watch her.

"A little help here," Vance called out.

The two other techs, Vance, and the deputy were still struggling with the body. There was no gurney aboard the boat and the body bag was proving hard to maneuver between land and sea, forcing them to use a backboard. The deceased had been a heavy man. Adding the weight of the body bag, the load was probably over three hundred pounds. Pierce and I went over to help, pausing to look back at Dick Tracy. He got the message and joined us.

The Miami-Dade crew stood waiting aboard. They hadn't left the boat, probably knowing their superiority would end on land. The techs retreated to the lighthouse with some muttered excuse that they weren't done processing the scene. The four of us carried the litter to the boat, slid it over the seawall, and placed it on the deck of the Miami-Dade Contender.

Then we stood there looking at each other. "We need to figure this out now. The gang thing is FBI territory." I looked over at Tracy and he nodded. No one in their right mind would want that one. Pierce nodded his assent—the FBI wasn't in their right mind. "For right now, let's leave the drugs with you guys," I said, looking at Tracy. Pierce was about to say something and I headed him off. "You'll share whatever evidence you find with the Feds." I had brokered a truce, but there was no telling how long it would last. "I'll handle the murder."

Wrapping up the crime scene was all procedure now. Justine had finished with the duffel, which was now placed inside a large bag to protect it and stowed on the Contender along with the body. Vance, Grace, and Tracy got aboard with the deputy. Glad to see them go, we released the lines and watched as they idled out of the harbor.

"You good?" I asked Justine.

"You know where to find me," she smiled.

Her boat idled away and I smiled to myself. "Get a ride back with you?" I asked Ray.

"Not right off. These dang bloodstains ain't going to wait for federal funding. Got to clean it up now."

That kind of thinking was just one of the reasons why Ray was indispensable. The barrier islands were constantly under assault from the elements. He knew what had to be done and when. "I'll give you a hand," I said. "Maybe we can fish tomorrow." With what we had just found, that was wishful thinking. As I helped him clean up the crime scene, I realized the blood would have never come off if we'd let the sun bake it.

We had finished the cleanup to his satisfaction and stepped down to the boat. With the lines tossed off, we idled out of the harbor. "You have a look at the body?" I asked.

Ray had gone back to the observation deck to have a look before the techs bagged the body.

"Yup. Outlaws for sure. Couldn't tell the rank from what was left. This ain't good, Kurt."

He didn't have to tell me what a gang war in the park would do. "So, the Outlaws lost the package they were either supposed to deliver or sell and the other gang killed one of their men in retribution, or you think there's more?"

"Could go like that," he said, pulling into a small cove off Elliot Key. "Got about an hour left on the tide. Seen some cobia cruising in here last week. You okay if we make a stop?

"Why not," I said. "It's not like we're on the clock." On top of that, with Martinez probably out playing some second-rate golf course, there was no one in his office to monitor my position. He had fine-tuned the art of surveilling his employees. Between the GPS trackers on the boat and truck, cameras at headquarters, three monitors on his desk, and the Cloud at his command, he knew where I was most of the time. But right now, there was really nothing else to do until the autopsy and forensics reports were in.

We cruised to a spot on the outside of Elliot Key I had never fished before. He dropped the anchor and let the boat drift back toward the mangroves. When it was about ten feet away, he snubbed the line.

We used the spinning rods he had already set up and stored in the console. He tied on white paddle-tail lures and after a brief explanation of how to fish them, we started casting toward the shore. On his first cast, Ray's rod bent over and he started to fight the fish. I could see the shadow running below the water as he turned the fish's head and guided it toward the boat. Once alongside, he reached down for the leader, hauled the thirty-inch fish over the gunwale, and with a smile tossed it into the cooler.

We tossed lures for the better part of an hour before he decided the tide was finished. Ray had pulled in another fish and I'd had one good hit that broke off in the mangroves. My attention had started to wane after the first few casts, and I was glad when he pulled the anchor. Ray was happy, but I was troubled.

I started to think about the gangs' presence in the park again on the way back to Adams Key. Murders are like jigsaw puzzles, with the corners being the motive, means, opportunity, added to some kind of an emotional or physical trigger. In many cases all three cornerstones exist before the perpetrator, and in many cases the victim of some wrongdoing, is pushed over the edge and actually kills. In this case, I had to throw it all out the window and come up with something else. Motive was simple; retribution, revenge, or just a cold-blooded killing. With gangs it really didn't matter. The location could cover both means and opportunity, though I had a feeling whoever had committed the murder had chosen the lighthouse to make a statement. The only reason to light the fire had been to attract attention. They were telling the government that they were now in charge.

That was as far as I had gotten when Ray pulled up to the dock at Adams Key. There was a handmade sign posted there, stating that the day use area was closed, and I suspected that Becky was taking some liberties with the shutdown in order to get some quiet. Zero came barreling down the dock like a bowling ball as Ray slid the boat against the dock. He reached into the cooler, grabbed the two fish we had kept by the gills and carried them to a concrete fish cleaning station off to the side, leaving me with the smaller mackerel. Zero followed him and sat at attention, hoping for some scraps. I offered to help and together we made short work of it. Then I went back to my house with four heavy Baggies to try and figure out my next move.

The clues were few: the duffel of drugs and the partially burnt colors of the dead man. Thinking of the deceased, I dialed the medical examiner's number. If it were my case, I would have to attend the autopsy. I thought that would be pretty cut and dry, and hoped Vance would, too.

"Hey, Kurt," he answered.

"What are you looking at for the autopsy?"

"I'm on my way out. I was going to give it to Sid to do tonight. I'll leave him a note to call you when he gets to it."

"Cool. What are you thinking?"

"We've had a whole lot of these gang-type killings lately. Cause of death doesn't really matter. Trying to find out who pulled the trigger, or in this case the knife, is the hard part. Those guys are good at covering for each other."

I thanked him. "Looks like I'll have some time on my hands with this shutdown. If you want to get out later this week, give a yell."

Relieved the autopsy was delayed, I hoped I could sway Sid to let me have a pass, though I knew the almost retired Jersey ME enjoyed my discomfort. Justine had the rest of the evidence, and I'd much rather see her anyway. Hoping my plan would work, I texted her and hopped in the shower.

Justine answered in the affirmative and an hour after Ray and I had pulled up to the dock, I was heading down the stairs from my stilt house. Ray, Becky, Jamie, and Zero were all gathered around a concrete grill beside their house and I smelled the butter and barbecue sauce mix that they used. Ray offered me a plate and I sat with them for a few minutes before I said a quick good-bye and headed to my boat.

Walking down the concrete walkway to the concrete dock, I thought about the blood-stained sidewalk and wondered what the park service fixation with the material was. Saltwater and concrete were not always a good mix. The steel rebar needed to reinforce the concrete rusted quickly when exposed to the marine environment, causing structural failure. The park service was known for over-building on the front end and being cheap on maintenance. The powers-that-be thought of the concrete as permanent and cost effective, and ignored the problems. It was just one of those things that I came in contact with every day that irritated me, but would probably survive the shutdown.

Going to meet Justine is a bit more complicated when there are seven miles of water between you and the park service headquarters in Homestead. Though technically off-duty, and dressed in cargo shorts and a T-shirt instead of my park service khakis, I still kept an eye on the boat traffic, hoping no one else would be taking advantage of the shutdown. It ended up being a typically quiet Monday, and I arrived at my slip twenty minutes after departing Adams Key.

After tying off, I walked past the building and thought about making a face at the security camera that was piped directly to Martinez's empty office. I restrained myself, knowing he'd spend the first few days back reviewing everything that had happened while he was gone. It was one of those ways he stayed on top of things and proved he was vital.

It was also a typical Monday on the highways of Dade County, and the traffic came to a halt several times due to the never-ending road construction. It wasn't too upsetting that the delays caused me to reach the crime lab just after five. The day crew had gone and I hoped Justine was by herself as I approached the entrance to the newly remodeled lab. Back in the day, I would have been able to watch her from the window in the hall of the old lab, until she inevitably sensed I was there. Now, I had to search her out.

"Hey!" I called out.

"Over here," she yelled back.

I followed her voice, passing banks of LED indicator lights on the latest in forensics equipment. I had no idea what most were used for. I found her and the first thing I noticed were the headphones she always listened to music with were gone. I knew this change was not good for her.

She had the denim vest laid out on a table and was scanning it with what looked like some kind of UV light.

"Lot of blood on this sucker."

"You think the perp's blood is there, too?" Knives were messy and often nicked the user as well as the victim.

"It's gonna take some time, but I'll run the DNA."

I moved closer, noticing immediately that she was uneasy when I pressed my hip against hers. This new lab was going to take some getting used to. I stepped back and watched as she scraped the burnt parts away from the sewn-on insignia. Parts had resisted the fire and before long I started to make out the lettering.

# 7

Gangs were a problem in Miami. Chicago and LA grabbed most of the headlines, but South Florida was in the top five worst areas, especially Dade County. The multi-cultured county had its share of neighborhood-related violence, but for the rest of us it was off our radar. Not so for the police who, along with the Feds, kept databases on members, tattoos, and anything else they could document. The Feds were especially good about this. Already known for being paper pushers, they excelled in collecting the documentation needed to prosecute under the RICO Act. If I wanted more information, I would need the help of Ron Pierce. Remembering he had given me a card, I found it in my pocket.

"Pierce," he answered.

I had figured him for an answer-the-phone guy. With every LEO officer having a smartphone, it had become prevalent to either text or use voicemail. Like everywhere else in our society, technology was pushing out human interaction. "Hey, it's Kurt Hunter. We got something on the colors from the lighthouse."

"They were burned pretty bad. Your tech must be good."

I stopped myself from saying she was the best. "Yeah, anyway, the colors are from the Outlaws."

"Interesting. Burning the colors is making a statement."

"Retribution for losing the drugs?"

"The one thing you can count on about bikers and gangs is that you can't count on them. Shoot from the hip is the way most roll."

"Kurt," Justine called from across the room.

With the phone still to my ear, I walked over beside her and looked up at the TV mounted on the wall. Why a forensics lab needed a dozen TVs and a coffee bar, I wasn't sure, but in this case it proved worthwhile. I asked Pierce to hold on while I watched Martinez, in his dress uniform, standing alongside the Miami-Dade police commissioner behind a table. Carefully staged in front of them to look like twice as much as I would have guessed was in the duffel bag, were the drugs we had found. The two men smiled and patted each other on the back as they took questions from the press.

"Turn on the news," I told Pierce. "Those bastards snaked us."

I had underestimated my boss. Thinking that without a paycheck he would ignore the park, I had instead discovered that he had used his surveillance network to get behind the podium, something I had learned was more important to him than money. This was not the first time I had thought about taking a page from the playbook of the criminals we chased and getting several burner phones in order to avoid him.

Between being angry and at the same time engrossed in the broadcast, I hadn't noticed Justine leave my side until I heard the vacuum seal of the evidence locker open. In place of the standard steel cage was a state-of-the-art, secured and air-conditioned vault. It really wasn't a vacuum seal, but the positive air pressure maintained by a separate air-conditioning system made a whoosh whenever the inch-thick glass doors were opened. She came back a minute later with the duffel and set it on the table.

"It's still here." Martinez and the commissioner had indeed staged the drugs. That made it better, but far from right. "They set up the whole thing. We still have the duffel and contents," I said into the phone. I wasn't sure if Pierce was still on the line.

"Typical. At least we have the real stuff."

"Yeah, but our element of surprise is gone." I had been plotting my next moves and the first thing I had planned was a bit of undercover work. Motorcycle clubs were bad about sending emails and newsletters. If you wanted to know what was going on, you had to find their hangout and for that I needed Pierce.

"The drugs are going to take a backseat to the murder. We might have just figured out which gang the victim belonged to, but they already know who it was. There's probably a heck of a wake going on somewhere."

Justine was beside me again, watching the news. She pointed to the screen, showing a street scene, the curbs lined with gleaming chrome. The camera moved to a reporter who was clearly not comfortable with this assignment. Justine turned up the volume. I told Pierce what network we were watching and set the phone on speaker before placing it on the counter.

"The Outlaw Motorcycle Club is out in full force tonight after a member of their club was murdered." The reporter looked over his shoulder and the camera panned to a group of leather-clad bikers coming toward him. "More to come," he squeezed in before the camera was jostled and the screen went black. The network feed went back to the studio and Justine turned down the volume as the talent on screen tried to explain that their reporter was fine.

"I know that bar. Did some undercover there," Pierce's voice came from the phone. "If you're up to it we can do a drive-by. If the natives aren't too restless, maybe we can get some info. You ride?"

"Some." I'd been riding bikes for years, though mostly off-road, I was comfortable with just about anything off the production line. Some of the custom or chopped bikes that club members used were out of my wheelhouse, however. The art of taking a stock bike and cutting weight at the same time as adding performance features was big business where *safety first* was not a concern. He gave me an address in North Miami Beach to meet him and I disconnected.

I caught Justine's look. "It'll be okay." I almost said it was because I was going with the FBI, but I didn't think that would help matters.

"I don't like it."

"Sorry, but ..." I shrugged, not knowing what to say. It was my job.

"Maybe I ought to go along and keep an eye on you," she said.

It wasn't a question, just a reminder. We had been together at the tail end of several cases before and she had saved my life once.

It was the culture of the clubs that I was worried about. My girl was hot and a badass, but they treated women badly in general and I would never put her in a compromising situation that I had no control over. Truth be told, I was apprehensive about going with Pierce.

She was lukewarm to my advances when I tried to kiss her before leaving, although I did get the okay to stay over later. Leaving the lab, I went out to the truck and entered the address in my phone, wondering if doing so would raise a red flag and alert Martinez. Apparently, his surveillance was more sophisticated than I had thought.

It was close to midnight when I left the lab. Pulling out of the parking lot, I took a left on NW 25th Street and hopped on the Palmetto Expressway heading north. The highway took a hard right and headed east after a few miles and when it intersected with I-95, I entered the northbound lanes. The lines between the cities blurred, with each looking the same, and I finally reached the 167th Street exit.

North Miami Beach was an old town that was trying to look new. Even at night, I could see restrictions had been added to the zoning codes, and the city had started requiring larger buffers, smaller signs, and more landscaping. Some blocks looked similar; the problem was where there was a mixture of old and new, the older buildings were set close to the road without a tree in sight. The difference became more noticeable when I turned off the main road and found myself in an industrial district.

My phone alerted me that I was at my destination, except I was looking at a narrow street, barely larger than an alley. It resembled a self-storage setup, with nothing but roll-up doors, but each door had an address and several buildings had office doors. Finally, I saw light coming from the bottom of one and pulled in front of it.

Pierce came out and directed me to a parking spot next to the sole tree on the block. I locked my truck and walked back. The space we entered was about twenty feet wide by fifty deep with a bathroom in back. Custom paint equipment lined one wall, and tool chests and a workbench the other. In the center of the space were a half-dozen motorcycles. Several were stripped down.

"Welcome to the FBI MC."

I looked over the bikes: all Harleys except for one Indian. I moved toward the latter, admiring the bike.

"Don't get too attached to that one. Find something to wear and we'll get out of here," he said, pointing to a pile of clothes in the corner.

They were dirty and oil stained, perfectly suitable for where we were going. I found a pair of jeans and a long-sleeved shirt that were close to my size, figuring I had better hide as much of my inkless skin as possible. After changing in the bathroom, Pierce pointed out the bike next to his. It was slightly smaller than the one he was on, but being used to crotch rockets and off-road bikes, it still seemed big to me. Pierce handed me a black helmet with a full face shield. He had a bowl type helmet and wore oversized glasses.

A minute later, we pulled out of the shop. Pierce closed the door and I followed him onto the road. It was a little intimidating at first. With the exception of one hair-raising ride from Key West to Miami several months ago, I hadn't ridden in more than a year. Following him through the city was a challenge. Pierce motioned me up in the lane, but I stayed back, not ready to ride bar to bar yet.

By the time we reached the Palmetto, I was in the groove and realized I was smiling. The feeling of freedom was something I had just started to get, like when my boat went up on plane and there was nothing but open water in front of me. I had gotten the same feeling of freedom riding through the trails of the Plumas forest.

Pierce turned off on Highway 41 and my smile faded as we rode west toward the Everglades. From my experience, nothing good happened out here, but the fringes of Dade County would be the perfect place for a biker bar. There was no hesitation on his part when we turned into a parking lot full of bikes. I recognized it from the news broadcast. Riding to the end of the row, we stopped and backed our bikes in line with the others. "Keep it cool. You don't mess with them, and they won't mess with you—especially the women. Don't even look."

I didn't need the warning. On the way to the bar, we passed clusters of people, both men and women, mostly smoking cigarettes, but I could smell weed in the air. Many were dressed as we were and not wearing colors, though from their tattoos and hardened expressions some looked like they should be. Pierce warned me that many were Outlaws out on probation. Wearing colors was a parole violation.

I kept my eyes down, trying not to show how uncomfortable I was. I'm a big guy at six feet and two-twenty-five. The guy at the door with a gallon jar stuffed with bills was me plus one. He thrust the jar at us, saying it was a collection for the deceased and I dug around in my pockets. I had a moment of panic when I realized I had left my wallet in my shorts back at the storage unit. I caught a mean look from the bouncer when Pierce bailed me out by dropping a twenty in the jar.

He bought a couple bottles of beer at the bar and we walked through the crowd trying to eavesdrop on any conversation that had anything to do with what had happened earlier. The talk was mostly about Cooker, whom I guessed was the deceased. The crowd seemed to be separated into groups: those wearing colors and those without. When we passed the former, I heard the word *retribution* several times. Pierce steered us away.

# 8

Pierce whispered some of their names in my ear as we cruised through the crowded bar. They were all nicknames: Motor, Grinder, Dirt, and anything else you could think of along those lines. I was more inclined to go with the Seven Dwarves: Sleepy, Grumpy, and Doc.

Doc turned out to be the president and I tried to keep an eye on him while absorbing as much of the scene as I could. He was small compared to some of the bikers. Most could easily have filled out the Dolphins' defensive line, and from the looks on their faces they had the killer instinct and would probably have performed better than the current roster. Doc moved through the crowd saying at least something to everyone he passed.

Clubs have rules, elections, and boards. To outsiders they might seem like a warlord society, but they rely heavily on protocol, and as the current federal shutdown had proven they are more effective at governing. Pierce guided us toward the leader in what looked like a random pattern, but after watching some of the men move around, I noticed he was avoiding some. When we got within a few feet of Doc, I saw him raise his eyes and look to the side of me, then nod to whomever was there.

I froze when two women stepped in front of us. Actually, just "women" was too general a term for them. They were leather-clad and hot. One made a move towards us and the alarm bells went off in my head. I was about to make for the door when I felt a hand grab my arm. Pierce signaled me with a look that running would be a bad idea. In the biker world, each of these women was either someone's old lady or a mama, what you might call a generalist. Snubbing them would lead to trouble. One slung her arm around my neck and I caught the flash of a camera as our picture was taken. Looking over at Pierce, who was in the same predicament, I gave him a questioning look, trusting him to take the lead. It proved unnecessary as a group of bikers approached us. The women disappeared and quickly blended back into the crowd. Pierce pushed me in front of him as we slid sideways through the packed bar. Once outside I finally took a breath as we moved past the groups smoking cigarettes, to the side of the building.

"What was that about?"

"I think they made you. Now our pictures are on the clubhouse wall."

"What about you?"

"They want custom paint work, they'll overlook a lot. Their bikes are their status symbols. You could live in a roach-infested studio apartment and they would all overlook it if your bike was tits. I've got a guy that works for me that's a freakin artist. Good cover."

"Shouldn't we get out of here?"

He looked back around the corner of the building and pulled his head back. "They're suspicious. Those guys are waiting outside. If we take off now, they'll follow us. Better to just hang out here for a few minutes and let them think they lost us."

"Why the interest? We look like half the other people in there."

"You've got to get past their looks. Sure, some are thugs, but the leaders, especially Doc, got where they are with brains and balls. For these clubs or gangs to even exist anymore they've got to be not only one step ahead of the Feds, but also the other gangs. They're shrewd."

I thought I might have been the one to blow our cover and felt bad. They had our pictures now, and whatever undercover work Pierce had done might be ruined. He seemed to dismiss the incident.

He looked back around the corner. "They're gone. Let's give it another minute and we'll take off."

Finally, Pierce and I started around the back of the building, staying to the poorly lit areas of the parking lot. The route took us away from the front of the building and we made it to our bikes without incident. I followed Pierce's lead as he settled onto the bike and put his helmet on. I felt less vulnerable once my helmet was on and started the engine, stepping backward until the front wheel was clear. I almost freaked out when Pierce goosed the throttle and heads turned toward us, but then realized this was expected behavior and it would have drawn more eyes if we had just slid into the night. The full face mask gave me a degree of anonymity I wasn't sure I should be feeling as we started out of the parking lot. It dawned on me after seeing the other helmets hanging from the other bikes that mine was the only one with a full mask. Many had ones similar to Pierce's or none at all.

With my head on a swivel, spending as much time looking into my mirror as I did watching the road, I followed Pierce back to the shop. After parking the bike where I had found it, I changed back into my clothes. Pierce stayed dressed in his leathers. Sitting at a table with a bottle in front of him, he leaned over and worked his phone, which was now connected by a short cable to the glasses he had worn.

"Holy crap," I said. "Secret agent shit."

"FBI at your service."

He had recorded everything we had seen in the bar, along with whatever audio the miniature microphone could grab over the music. We watched the faces while listening to the heavy metal soundtrack.

"Wait. That's two of the guys from the crabber."

He stopped the video and zoomed in on the two men. "Nobody I know, but that doesn't mean much. It's pretty common to bring help down from some of the clubs up north who won't be recognized here when they are making a move."

"I didn't realize they were so well organized." My preconceived notion of motorcycle clubs was an image of the Hell's Angels' infamous runs—mostly just wild parties until the drugs and alcohol ran out, or until the locals brought them to a violent end.

"If there was a Fortune 500 listing for gangs, these guys would be in the top ten."

"I thought it was mostly a weekend thing now." It had taken a whole lot of contractors, doctors, lawyers, and accountants to fuel the resurgence of the Harley-Davidson Company. In the late sixties they'd been selling ten to fifteen thousand bikes a year. By 2000, it was over twenty times that.

"There's still the hardcore element, and it's grown as well. In the sixties there were probably only a couple of thousand bikers out there. Their tattoos, piercing, and facial hair weren't accepted and they couldn't find work, so crime was it. While the whole Harley thing has grown, the one percent mentality and outlaw life has blossomed with it."

"And with local law enforcement not recognizing the out-of-town help and a hundred of their best friends providing alibis, it's hard to make any arrests." I stated the obvious.

It all made sense. I focused again on the group. "Can we do anything with the audio?"

"I'll need a computer for that. I can email you the file."

That would have been great, except for the Cloud. Martinez had access to everything that went through my phone. "Any chance of a putting it on a flash drive?"

"No problem, but it'll have to be tomorrow when I can grab one from the office."

"Okay." I glanced down at my watch, realizing it was after two. It was a rare occurrence when I was still awake when Justine got off work, and I had an invitation to her apartment. I felt a surge of energy. "I'm gonna take off then. I'll call you tomorrow."

"Right. Sorry about the excitement tonight."

"Just part of the game."

I left the shop and hopped into the park service truck. When I reached Justine's I noticed her car was not there. Thinking she would be home anytime, I locked the truck and used my key to let myself into her apartment. It had been a big moment when she had given me the key. I had called that level five in our relationship. Since then, we had gone a couple steps higher—she had given me a drawer in her dresser.

I sat down on the couch with a bottle of beer and started to fight off the inevitable. My body was exhausted and my shoulders were tight from the stress. I decided to hang out on the couch instead of the bed to gain any advantage I could to stay awake. My eyes had just started to close when I heard the door open, and I jumped up.

"Hey, didn't mean to wake you," Justine said.

"I was up."

"Right. Not to deter you from the planned activity, but I got something off that vest."

She had my attention on both fronts. I sat up and stretched, fighting the urge to rub my eyes, which would concede that I had been asleep. Justine sat next to me and opened up her laptop. On the screen were pictures of the semi-burnt vest. I saw the colors, and a few patches. There was no specific rank, nickname, or anything else that I could see other than the club name and a one percent patch that, depending who you asked, either meant you were part of the counterculture or that you had killed someone.

"I'm not seeing anything."

"I started playing with some of the new toys in the lab. There is a handheld laser detector that analyzes fibers for trace materials. I was trying to isolate the accelerant, and came up with some kind of propionate. I have to run some more tests to identify it. The bar graph on the right shows the readout from the vest."

I looked closer this time and saw the list of *ingredients*. There were some I recognized and others I didn't. Not in the mood for a chemistry lesson, I let it go, thinking it would be better to get the full report. She must have read my mind.

"We'll check the drugs tomorrow. I left the duffel you found for the day crew to analyze. I'm still learning how to use some of this new equipment."

I saw something in Justine that had been missing since she had been *evicted* from her small downstairs lab and forced to move upstairs into the new lab. She had even talked about a transfer. This was the first time she seemed genuinely excited to be working again.

Maybe I should have gone to bed when I'd arrived here, because it turned out that would have been my only chance to sleep. Just as Justine finished her summary, my phone vibrated. I looked down at the screen and saw Ray's name. For him to be calling this time of night, something must be really wrong. I picked it up and pressed ACCEPT.

"Hey, you guys okay?"

"That freakin' dog is killing me, but his barking paid off this time. There was a boat that pulled up to the dock. Crabber, from the look of it. I saw some of those biker guys aboard. Shotgun scared them off, though." I thanked him and disconnected. It looked like Zero was going to cost both of us a night's rest. I looked at my watch and saw it was already three-thirty. I decided to waive whatever sleep I might still get and head back to the island.

Justine must have seen the look on my face. "Go on if you have to," she said.

"I'm sorry. I'll make it up to you." I regretted the words as soon they were out of my mouth. This wouldn't be the first time I had put work ahead of our relationship and it probably wouldn't be the last. I could only hope there'd be no lasting damage. I offered an ill-timed peace offering. "Hey. Mariposa wants us to come over for dinner again. How about this weekend?" Working the reception desk at headquarters, the matronly Jamaican was my sole ally there.

"So, lure me in with some Jamaican rum. Just remember how that ended last time."

The Appleton 21 that Mariposa's husband was only allowed to have with guests had been outstanding that night, as well as the dinner. The only problem was that we had been called away by a distress message from Susan McLeash. "Yeah, that. Can I tell her okay?"

"I won't hold this business against her, but you're going to pay for it. Now get going before I change my mind."

I kissed her hard, and reconsidered for a moment if I was doing the right thing. After the warning shot from Ray, I doubted the men from the crabber would be back, but I wasn't going to leave him and his family out there alone if they returned. Adams Key and the park were my home. I had come to respect the park's ecosystem and I took my responsibility to protect it seriously. "Call you later."

I left quickly and headed to the truck. Several times I looked over my shoulder, wondering if I was being Don Quixote and if I should just turn around and do what any sensible guy would do. Instead I continued to the truck, and with a feeling of foreboding started toward headquarters.

# 9

I WAS EDGY, A MIXTURE OF BEING TIRED AND ANXIOUS. SEVERAL TIMES I found myself pushing eighty and had to slow down as I headed south on the Turnpike. Between the construction and the ever-present lowriders with their bass booming and going faster than I was, I tried to stay focused. The late night traffic here was dicey. It was hard to believe in the darkest hours of the night, after the bars had closed and before the earliest commuters had hit the road, they would not think themselves prime targets. Just as I thought this I saw flashing red, white, and blue lights ahead, and when I slowed I saw that an FHP cruiser had pulled over the van that had just blown by me. They were parked on the side of the road in front of the police car. Both doors were open and two men were spreadeagled on the shoulder.

I slowed further when I saw the gang colors, and pulled onto the shoulder. I parked by some construction equipment in front of the van, and hoped that the officer had gotten a look at the insignia on the side of the truck, which was more visible than the junior ranger light bar on top. It was so small it was often confused for a roof rack. I had barely gotten the door open when I heard the officer yell.

"Stay where you are."

"Special Agent Kurt Hunter with the Parks Service," I called back, raising my hands over my head.

"Are you armed?"

"No."

"ID?"

I reached slowly for my wallet, pulled it out of my back pocket, and opened it. The beam of his light caught my eyes and he stepped closer for a better look. I was regretting my decision now if for no other reason than that I was distracting him from the two men. My instincts proved correct when the men took off at a run toward the construction area, where it looked like an overpass was being built. The officer gave me a disgusted look and called after them. They ignored the standard warning and, figuring I was in enough trouble with yet another agency, I took off at a run after them.

I heard him call after me, and glanced back to see him about fifty yards behind. The area adjacent to the highway was flat and open, making it easy to see the two men. I was about a hundred yards behind and felt my breath shorten. Sucking air, I started falling behind and cursed myself for being out of shape. The extra adrenaline feeding their muscles also helped the escaping men distance themselves. I was running after them; they were running from jail.

The officer caught up with me just as the men reached a group of containers and construction equipment where they would easily be able to hide. Giving up the chase I stood there bent over with my hands on my hips, breathing heavily and ready to take my beating.

"Y'all park service boys don't do much PT, do you?"

I turned to look at the trooper, standing a few inches taller than I was. I could tell by the set of his shoulders that he wasn't a stranger to the gym, and he was barely out of breath.

"I called for backup. They should be here any minute. Those guys think they're slick, but they're on an island here. We'll get them."

We were standing in a large area between the north- and southbound traffic lanes. He was right; there was no way out without crossing the highway. "Sorry about that." I had turned a routine traffic stop into a multi-unit chase.

"Shoot, this time of night, it's something to do. Those guys were acting suspicious as hell. I had already called one backup unit." He paused, looking back as a cruiser pulled off the highway behind his car. He called them on the radio, asking them to move to the next exit and circle back on foot. They pulled back onto the highway and he turned to look at me. I almost wished it was daylight so his sunglasses would hide the piercing look he gave me.

"What's your interest in this? Don't think I have ever had a NPS dude pull over to help before."

Before I could respond, two more cars pulled up and he gave them orders. Within minutes, there were police cars at the corners of the construction site. The officers were on foot now, and closing in on the area the men were hiding. I followed the trooper in front of me, staying far enough back that I wouldn't interfere with the operation—again.

Slowly the ring closed around the suspects and the trooper in front of me called out to them. There was a moment's silence and then one of the men yelled that they were coming out. A minute later, the two men walked out side by side with their hands over their heads. They waited patiently while the troopers tightened the circle and finally two approached the men, kicked out their feet, and pushed them to the ground. Seconds later, they were in cuffs and being frog-marched toward the highway.

"So, you never said why you stopped."

This was my first interaction with the highway patrol, and after dealing with Miami-Dade for the past year I was surprised by how friendly they were. "Had a murder out at Boca Chita Key the other day. Looks like gang activity. I saw the colors on the men you pulled over and thought I might see what was up."

"Well, that didn't turn out too well," he said, extending his hand. "Jim Stallworth."

"Mind if I see which gang they're from?"

"Nope. Might as well help. Since they took off, I've got enough cause to search their vehicle now. You might have done me a favor."

The men were complaining that the cuffs were too tight, which only encouraged the two officers leading them to wedge their nightsticks harder against the men's arms. They reached Stallworth's cruiser and dropped the men in the back seat. Once the automatic locks on the doors were engaged, they were contained and the tension dropped.

"Who's your buddy, Jim?"

The least I could do was divert the ridicule they were going to dish out. I introduced myself and shook their hands.

"Little far from the water?" one asked.

I retold the story of the crabber and the murder at the lighthouse, figuring there was no harm. They might run across something and help my investigation. To that end, I handed all three men my card.

"Outlaws are causing a lot of trouble. I work mostly south county and I've seen a lot of action. It looks like they're making a move," Stallworth said.

"With the government shutdown and all, are they smart enough to move their business out to the park?"

The troopers worked for the state of Florida and were likely unaffected by the political posturing in DC. Stallworth looked at the men in the back seat. "They might look like a bunch of unwashed bikers, but they are extremely organized. Some of these chapters have been fighting the Feds trying to throw RICO in their faces for years. They always seem to make it go away."

"Thanks. Do you know these two?"

"Look like just soldiers to me. Outlaws for sure, by their colors." He walked to the window and looked at the two men. "Don't recognize them, but I hear they're bringing in out of town help. Word on the street is that something's going down."

"I think it's started already." I explained about the setup at the lighthouse.

"That'd be Doc. He's president of the Outlaws local chapter. Crafty dude."

I remembered him from the bar. "Saw him last night."

He gave me a questioning look.

"I was with an FBI agent, undercover. We went to some bar out west of Kendall."

He gave a quick description of Pierce. "I think I know that dude. He's a little close to the action, if you know what I mean."

A call came over all three men's radios at the same time. Stallworth told the men he had this, and they took off. That left the two of us alone on the highway with the contained bikers.

"I'm gonna do a quick search of their vehicle. Maybe find something that we can hold them on for more than an hour. Stick around and help if you want."

I wasn't going to say no to that offer and waited by the side of the van. Stallworth came back a minute later with gloves and bags. He handed me a pair, which I put on, and I waited for him to take the lead.

He took the driver's side and I went to the passenger's. Starting with the visors, we worked our way down to under the seats, then finding nothing that could be used against the men we moved to the cargo area. It was set up like a mechanic's van, with shelves on either side. Boxes labeled with tool manufacturers' names were stacked neatly and held in place with bungee cords.

"I'm willing to bet they don't have tools in them."

Stallworth climbed in and removed a red plastic box with the name *Milwaukee* stenciled in white script across it. He brought it to the side door where I was standing. He spun the box so the clasps faced me. "You can have the honors."

I held my breath and opened the two clasps holding the lid shut and raised the cover. I wasn't sure what to expect, but when we saw the shotgun nestled neatly in a custom foam lining, we knew there was more. After opening several more boxes we had found some shells, another gun, and a large baggie of white powder. The two men in the back of the trooper's car were going to jail.

"There you go, your first break," Stallworth said.

I wasn't so sure about that. Gang members were famous for having tight lips and doing time rather than making a deal. It was a badge of honor to do a few years rather than rat out your brothers. The boxes were another matter. I would have liked to finish inspecting them now, but knew there was valuable forensic evidence to be found if I left them for the techs.

"Where do you take them?" I asked, not sure whether FHP had any kind of detention facility.

"Everybody goes to county."

With the turf war that had already started, that would complicate things. "You have a contact, or do you just run them in?"

"Usually just call the duty sergeant and they take care of the handoff."

I needed to make a decision while I still had some control of the situation. There were two choices: Ron Pierce or Grace Herrera. In theory, getting the FBI involved should be the best option, but from what I had seen of Pierce's interaction with Miami-Dade I wasn't sure. They were certainly capable of burying this to spite him. Instead, I decided to call Herrera.

I checked my watch. The sky had lightened and the surrounding area was turning a light grey as the sun made its move toward the horizon. It was early, but I pressed CONNECT and waited. The call went to voicemail, which I guessed was better than waking her up. I left a message and disconnected.

"I'm off at seven. Have to take out the trash before then." He looked over at the men. "Tow's on its way already."

The wheels of justice were running on shift time. "No worries. I just called a detective friend of mine at Miami-Dade. I'm hoping she can handle the intake."

"I gotta hang here until the tow truck comes. You've got that long to figure it out."

For once, I prayed for traffic. The northbound lanes had started to slow down with early commuters, but the southbound lanes were clear and a minute later a flatbed truck came from that direction and pulled onto the shoulder.

"You're out of time," Stallworth said.

The driver handed him a clipboard. Stallworth signed the form, and the man connected the winch. I heard the whine of the motor as it started pulling the van onto the bed. After ratcheting the tie downs, he waved at Stallworth. I watched as his tires spit the gravel from the shoulder as he pulled onto the turnpike. Stallworth turned to me and I was about to concede when my phone rang.

## 10

"Can you give me ten minutes? I've got a Miami-Dade detective on the way." Grace had jumped at the opportunity for the arrest. I didn't think it was about the credit—that wasn't her style—and guessed it was more of a pissing match with the FBI. I had dealt with mainly smaller jurisdictions out west, where the county sheriff's department looked more like a small town police force. Even with their limited resources they were always happy to see the FBI and other federal agencies leaving town.

"No problem. That'll take an hour of paperwork off my plate." He looked up at the sky. "Looks like the wind is down. You fish, Hunter?"

That conversation could have occupied more than the ten minutes it took for Grace to reach the site. It turned out he was more of an offshore fisherman, targeting dolphin and sailfish. That wasn't in my wheelhouse, but it didn't mean I wasn't interested.

"What'd you stumble on this time, Hunter?" Grace's partner asked.

I ignored him and helped Stallworth transfer the prisoners into Miami-Dade's custody and waive the ticket, figuring they were in enough trouble. We shook hands and he quickly hit the road. I watched as he turned on the light bar, navigated through the confused commuters and made a quick U-turn. At least someone was going fishing today.

"How do you want to play this?" Grace asked.

"It's your arrest. I've got nothing tying these guys to what happened in the park."

"I'll keep you in the loop."

"Appreciate that. The evidence should be interesting."

I chalked the incident up to my future karma with Miami-Dade, hoping the forensics would help me out in the murder investigation. Grace and her partner pulled into traffic and I stood alone on the shoulder of the Turnpike suddenly feeling very tired. I'd been up for twenty-four hours and remembered the call from Ray about our guests on the island last night.

If they were still out there, the best shot I had to find them now was to sit off one of the channels they would need to transit when they headed back south. Whether their purpose had been to scare me or worse, they hadn't succeeded.

I'd always had trouble sleeping during the day and thought about Stallworth, who was probably hooked up to his boat by now and heading to the ramp. The time clock was shut off and there was no reason I couldn't soak a line and decided to check out the Featherbed banks. I wasn't sure about the fishing, but had seen boats there before. It was as good a spot as any from where I could keep an eye on the bay if the crabber was still out there.

Coming from a stream-fishing background, I've been surprised at how different saltwater is. In moving water, the flow and temperature are the two big variables. Both are easy to observe. In the bay waters you have to consider the changing tides and how they're influenced by the phase of the moon as well as the wind, cloud cover, and temperature. Even if you're fly fishing, the bait needs to be located because that's where the fish are. I'd had heard Chico and some of the other guides speculating endlessly about where the bait would be. With the thousands of acres comprising Biscayne Bay, it was like a chess match.

I had formulated my strategy by the time I reached headquarters, and I left the truck behind the building. It was strange seeing the empty parking lot on a weekday and I instinctively lowered my head when I passed the security camera on the corner. I almost felt sorry for Martinez as I approached the next camera in his surveillance chain. This one covered the dock. The longer the shutdown lasted, the more video he would have to watch.

I half expected to see a chain locking my boat to the dock at some point, but there was nothing untoward as I stepped aboard. After starting the engine, I released the lines and idled back into the turning basin. The fuel was low, and I headed toward the pumps at the marina by Bayfront Park. I knew the attendant, but noticed as he handed me the nozzle that he was reserved. "I got this," I said. After sticking the spout into the fuel inlet, I reached into my pocket and removed my wallet. I could see he was relieved I was not going to try and charge the fuel to the NPS account that I assumed was frozen.

Filling up at a marina was at least a dollar more per gallon than land-based pumps, and after topping the tanks I was shocked to see I had taken seventy gallons, totaling over two hundred-fifty dollars. I had never noticed before. With no paychecks coming and the fees for my attorney, Daniel J. Viscount, having left my bank account in three figures after my custody hearing, I would have to start conserving my resources. Boats were not fuel efficient by nature and I changed the display on the fuel gauge to show current consumption. I'd never bothered to find the sweet spot between conservation and speed before, but now I realized the seven-mile trip home could cost twenty bucks if I ran the engine at full throttle. I settled on another fifteen minutes and half the gas.

After clearing the last channel marker, I started thinking as I sped across the light chop. Again the organization of the club surprised me. It had been less than a day since the body and drugs had been discovered and they knew I was the investigating officer and where I lived. The setup at the bar last night came to mind.

Zero was standing on the dock reassuring me that despite the shutdown things were normal here. Ray's boat was gone and I guessed he was doing what he always did. He was a creature of habit, and I doubt even the politicians could change his path. Becky came out and I watched her grab Jamie as he tried to mount Zero.

"Hey, Kurt, hear anything?"

I wondered if Ray had told her about our visitors. "Nah, headquarters is deserted and I haven't listened to the radio."

"Hope it don't go on too long. You're lookin' a little rough, everything okay?"

"Yeah, just working a case. Been up all night."

"You and Ray both. That pencil pusher Martinez don't know what he has with you two. I bet he ain't workin'."

I didn't want to go down this path with her. "I'm gonna grab a pole and head out for a bit."

"There ya go. Ray's out checkin' our traps, too. Maybe get some lobster we can sell."

Knowing the boundaries of the park like the lines on his hands, Ray knew exactly where to place his traps to catch the protected park lobster when they moved and crossed the invisible line. I suspected that he sold some on the black market, but I wasn't going to rat him out. Without him, the outer islands would be reclaimed by the sea.

"Just gonna hang out around Featherbed Banks."

"That ain't the spot if you're really fishing," she said.

I caught her suspicious look, but let it go. After petting Zero and playing with Jamie for a minute, I headed back to the house. The couch looked inviting, but I knew whatever sleep I got would be restless and short-lived. There was too much going through my mind. I filled a small cooler with some ice, a few waters, and a six-pack, finally grabbing my spinning rods on the way out. I had started out fly fishing because that's what I knew, but once I had learned to catch bait, if I wanted to fill up my freezer, the spinning rods were the ticket.

I paid my respects to Zero on my way to the boat, loaded up, dropped the lines, and headed out. It was a comfortable morning and I pulled up to the near side of the banks and dropped the Power-Pole. Once in place, I stared at the clear turquoise water. I'm not sure whether I was melancholy because of lack of sleep or because of the bodies I had found in this pristine water, but I just sat on the gunwale and watched the turtle grass swaying in the current for a few minutes. My plan had been to chum up some baitfish, which I would catch on a multi-hook Sabiki rig. Ray had tried to teach me the art of the cast net, but throwing one had so far eluded me.

The bug went deep with me. I was exhausted, but there was no fighting the urge. If there was water, I needed a line in it. After a few minutes, I went to the console and retrieved a baggie of Tropical fish food. Mixing a small amount of water into it, I started tossing clumps into the water. It didn't take long for the small fish to find it, and a minute later there was a school beside the boat. Dumping the rest of the contents in the water, I went for my rod, but before I could attach a weight to the end, I saw the telltale smoke and the faint sound of an old diesel engine on the wind. The crabber was coming back.

I did hesitate and watched the baitfish for a minute, trying to decide how far I should go on my own time and gas money. But these people had come to my island. My conscience overrode everything else. This was my home and if there was illegal activity going on in the park, I was going to stop it. I took one last glance at the fish swimming below the boat and put away the rod. Back at the helm, I simultaneously started the engine and lifted the Power-Pole. If I wanted to see where the crabber was from, I needed to get out of its way. If they were looking for me, a park service boat hanging out here during a government shutdown was too much of a coincidence.

Keeping an eye on the fuel gauge, I ran south, heading straight for the channel running through Cutter Bank. Beyond lay Card Sound and North Key Largo, what I called the wild west of the bay. It was an isolated area strewn with mangrove-lined coves on the inaccessible mainland, and protected on the eastern side from the Atlantic Ocean by what was commonly known as a smugglers' haven.

The water narrowed here and I quickly spun the wheel to port and headed for a small creek I knew in the mangroves. I entered Anglefish Creek and slid into the first side channel. This was where I had first met Johnny Wells when we had taken down a shrimper trying to offload square grouper. Concealed by the mangroves, I waited.

I was out of my comfort zone now and watched the telltale smoke pass by. This was a desolate area, with only the Card Sound Bridge, the less-traveled alternate entrance to the Keys, ahead. I moved out of the creek mouth and, giving the crabber a comfortable margin, began to follow. There was only one way through Card Bank and the bridge, so I dropped back.

When the crabber was well through Card Bank I picked up speed to follow. Ahead I could see the span of the bridge and to the right I saw a low building. It must have had a parking lot because though I couldn't see the vehicles, I could see the sun's reflection off the glass and chrome. The crabber was heading right toward it. I dropped back again and studied the chartplotter, pressing the option to show marinas and ramps. An icon displayed on the screen in the area where I saw the activity ahead and I zoomed in to read the label. It was Alabama Jacks.

The famous roadside eatery had been on my *take Justine there* list, but we hadn't made it yet. I crossed under the bridge and entered the canal running parallel to the road. As I approached the restaurant, I realized the glints of sunlight I had seen from the water were the reflection from the chrome off a row of at least twenty motorcycles. Right in front, tied to a wooden dock, was the crabber. As I approached I saw another forest green T-top and thought it might be Ray selling his catch. I approached to tie off next to him, and noticed the hull was newer. Between that and the configuration of the antennas on the T-top, I knew I was looking at Susan McLeash's boat.

## 11

Finding out what Susan had been up to would be easy work. All park service equipment was equipped with a GPS tracking chip and I had the code for her boat from one of her previous misadventures. It would be a simple matter to look up her movements over the last few days. There was always the chance she was innocent, though if her past behavior was an indicator, she was up to something. I remembered having to remove the dock line for her boat to get at mine the other day and had wondered about it then. It wasn't my job to watch her, but she had clearly used the boat at least twice after being reassigned. With her history, that was a red flag. Once I was through here I would have a look.

I turned my attention to the crabber. The crew looked familiar, and I pulled my phone from the waterproof compartment below the helm and scrolled through the pictures I had taken yesterday. The men unloading unmarked boxes from the crabber were the same ones that had been aboard the other day. While I had the phone out, I switched to the camera and started taking pictures of the activity on the dock.

Four men were doing the heavy work; unloading the boat and placing the boxes in an unmarked panel van that could have been a twin of the one Stallworth had pulled over. Several other men were standing by with their hands inside their vests. I couldn't see the weapons, but they were definitely there. Another two men were sitting in the shade at a nearby table, drinking beer and watching. I recognized one as Doc, the president that I had seen the other night. He was the only one dressed in colors. The man next to him was fitted out in the latest fishing fashion. He had his back to me and from here I could see the outline of a machine gun and the name of a shooting range embroidered on the back of the shirt. Even dressed like this in Florida, he looked out of place, and I suspected he'd never held a rod before. If the club was dealing in weapons it made sense that they had someone local. This looked like a business transaction to me.

I had the boat wedged between two large mangroves. With Susan's park service boat already tied to the dock, I wasn't worried about the boat being seen, but if I were recognized, that might be another issue. After the incident at the biker bar with the women and pictures, then their visit to Adams Key last night, I knew I was on their radar—not a place I wanted to be.

If I was going to leave the boat here, I would have to wade across the canal. That would surely attract attention. The only option was to use the dock. I pulled out of the brush and backed the boat behind Susan's, thinking she might actually be useful in providing an excuse for me to be here. That would require a degree of civility, but I could fake my role. I only hoped she would act the same. After tying off, I climbed the dock and scanned the outside seating area.

There she was sitting by herself, but there were two bottles of beer on the table. I was on my way toward her when I saw Ron Pierce coming from the bathrooms. My gut told me there was something wrong here and I ducked behind a section of lattice beside the building. I hate being right when it complicates things and that is exactly what happened when Ron sat at the table with Susan. I wasn't sure what kind of game he was playing, but with Susan McLeash involved, I expected the worst.

I watched them through the diagonal slats of wood. It was immediately obvious from their interaction that Pierce was using her. Even if I wasn't aware of her tendency toward drama, it was easy to read Susan's body language—they were sleeping together. The question was what was he getting out of it, because he was clearly disinterested in her. His chair was positioned so he could see the table with Doc and the other man, and he watched them as he responded offhandedly to whatever Susan was babbling about. She clearly thought she had scored and didn't notice that every woman that walked by caught his eye.

I'd wondered earlier how he'd found out about the murder on Boca Chita so quickly and so casually arrived on the scene. Susan would likely still have access to the park service computers and with her relationship with Martinez, she could probably access his surveillance feed. Couple that with the trackers on my boat, truck, and cell phone, and I suspected Martinez wasn't the only one keeping an eye on me.

There was nothing to be gained by being seen by them, and I turned my attention to the crabber and bikers. The men continued to unload the crabber and I realized I had to do something quickly or the opportunity would be lost. We were south of the park boundary and out of my jurisdiction. Had I seen the crabber take on its load inside the park, I would have some leeway into what I did, but without even an incident being reported, I was powerless. I'd danced with the NPS manual before and knew that I had the authority to follow up on crimes committed inside the park wherever they led. This had caused friction with the local authorities several times, but they had nothing to worry about this time. I would play by the rules.

I looked back at Susan and Pierce and wondered what he was doing here and why he was with her. Somehow, he'd known the meet was here. My best guess was that it was through his contacts inside the club. His tentacles seemed to reach everywhere. Whatever his agenda, appearing here with an LEO officer, even if it was Susan, was brilliant.

Thinking about the tracking capabilities gave me an idea. It struck me that if Susan had been able to track me that I could use the same technology to follow the van. I already knew where the chip and tag were on my boat. As long as I could remain out of sight, I had nothing to lose and decided the risk was worth the reward. I moved away from my hiding spot and stayed out of sight as I made my way back to the boat. Glancing over at the crabber, I noticed the men were taking a break. A rental convertible pulled next to their bikes and three women exited the car. Their heads turned and I quickly hopped aboard, started the engine, and released the lines.

Not really worried about concealing myself or the boat before, I had taken the last spot at the floating dock in the wide-open canal. Now, I needed to move. Dropping the throttle into reverse and staying close to the mangroves I slowly idled backward until I was far enough away to turn without being seen. The men didn't look like they were in a rush, but I guessed after studying the chartplotter that it would take every bit of ten minutes to cross under the bridge and hide the boat in the mangroves on the other side of the road.

The brush was thick, causing me to strain to see through the mangroves as I idled down the canal on the opposite side of the road. Finally, I glimpsed the side of the van and pulled into a slot between several large bushes. After tying the boat to a few of the larger branches I reached into the console for the fillet knife I carried.

The flexible blade was perfect for removing the tracking tag. With it in my pocket, I slid off the bow, careful to keep my feet on the exposed roots as I wove through the tangled maze to the road. Without my uniform I was just another tourist, and with my head down just in case I was recognized from last night, I crossed the road, walked past the row of bikes, and approached the van.

The one thing you could usually count on with gangs was that they were cocky. The premise that there was safety in numbers was one of their key tenets. It might work in a fight, but it slowed things down otherwise. There was a casual attitude among the men. They were still lounging around drinking beer and smoking. I couldn't tell if it was weed or cigarettes, and didn't care.

I continued toward the passenger side of the van, which faced the street and was out of their line of sight. Casually, I pretended to admire the bikes as I walked along the road. I made it to the van and relaxed, knowing the solid sides blocked the men's view of me. But that worked two ways, and I couldn't see them either.

I was committed now, and walked casually to the passenger door and breathed out again when I found it unlocked. Easing it open enough for me to reach my hand in, I pulled the tracker from my pocket and slid my arm inside. The first contact was a sticky substance. I sucked in a breath and moved further in, looking for a place to hide the tracker. My hand brushed against empty beer bottles and food wrappers. I finally settled on placing the device underneath the floor mat. From the debris on the floorboards I doubted the van would be cleaned anytime soon. Releasing my breath, I pulled my hand out, gently closed the door and continued walking along the road.

There was nothing to do but wait until they left and I made my way back to the boat and leaned against the console. It took seconds for the first cloud of mosquitos to zero in on me. With nothing else to do, I pulled out my phone. I had turned off the ringer and vibrator earlier and now, looking at the screen, I saw several messages.

I put the phone back on vibrate only and scanned through the notifications, and stopped scanning when I came upon one from Allie. It was three letters that had become her standard greeting—SUP. I answered with a quick hello and that I was looking forward to seeing her this weekend. We were planning another trip down to TJ's dive shop. I had a moment of remorse when the latest sign of decay presented itself—I had to squint at to see the detail of the emoji, finally deciding that it was a smiley face. Grace had left a text to call her. She was a phone person and only texted to get my attention. The call back would have to wait.

The phone vibrated and a text from Justine came through. Before giving her all my attention, I quickly scanned the rest of the messages. One had several pictures of a large dolphinfish from a number I didn't know. When I scrolled through them, I saw Stallworth holding a fish in each hand. They were easily three feet long and I wondered if he might extend another invitation to go out with him. I had almost said yes this morning. The next one, I wouldn't turn down.

I drank some water and slapped at my exposed skin. There was nothing I could do except try and fight off the mosquitos and wait. My eyes were blurry and I had a headache from the lack of sleep. The last day and a half was taking its toll.

Unable to see the road, I had to rely on my hearing. There were several false alarms as single or small groups of bikes sped by. It didn't take long to tell these riders from the bikers across the street when they stopped just up the road for the toll and then took off again. Finally, a loud roar came through the brush as the bikers revved their throttles before heading out. I waited, scratching the bites on my neck until the sound of the bikes faded as they headed back to Florida City.

I assumed the van had gone with them. It would have no choice but to follow Card Sound Road back to Florida City, which gave me a few minutes and I picked up my phone thinking it was safe to talk now. I opened Justine's message. She must have just gotten to work and wanted me to call. I hoped she had been assigned to the truck that had been impounded this morning.

"Hey," I started.

"You better make a date now, because I may never get out of here. That was quite the haul this morning."

"What'd you find?"

"I'm just getting started, but there are all the usual suspects: drugs, guns, and ammo."

The only other pillars of criminal activity missing were prostitution and gambling, neither of which would fit in a tool box. "Want me to come down?"

"I'm upstairs in the new lab. Too many people here for you to be hanging around. You're buddy Dick Tracy's been by a few times to look over my shoulder, too."

"What'd he want?"

"Never got that far after I elbowed him in the stomach."

That's my girl. "Okay, I'll check in later. I've got to get some sleep."

"Cool, leave me to pick up after you again."

Even though she laughed when she said it, I wondered if there was any truth to it. I'd reached down to start the engine when I remembered Grace had wanted me to call her. Leaning back again, I hit her number and waited. Her calls often went to voicemail, but she answered right away.

"Hey, Kurt. We processed those two thugs from this morning. Turns out they're Outlaws. One of them wants to make a deal. We're going to interview him in a few if you want to sit in."

"Can you hold that for a few hours? I've got something else I may be able to pass to you if you can give me some time."

"If it's as good as this guy, I'll take it. We can put him on ice. Probably get more out of him after he sweats it out in an interview room for a few hours. Just so you know—he asked for you."

## 12

I leaned back against the console with the phone in my hand, waiting for an internet connection so I could track the van. I had only done this one time before, after Susan McLeash had gone rogue during a case, and once it connected it took me a few minutes to fumble through the screens. To make matters worse, my head was pounding and my bloodshot eyes were blurry. My brain was in a fog and my problem-solving abilities were fading.

I finally navigated to what I thought was the correct screen, but when I entered my tracking number, I got an error message. Susan's came back with the same result. A quick shot of paranoia fueled adrenaline brought my level of consciousness out of the gutter and I stared at the screen, wondering what had happened.

I tried several more times with the same result. Anger is better than coffee, and my brain was starting to work again. I had to do something I usually avoided at all costs or my afternoon's work would be in vain. I had another decision to make: Pierce or Martinez. The FBI would have the resources to track the chip from its barcode. Martinez certainly could and might be watching now. If I hadn't seen Pierce with Susan earlier he would have been the first call. Instead, I dialed Martinez.

He smelled the podium as soon as I explained the chip was attached to a van filled with drugs. Any repercussions I had been expecting for going off the reservation were on the back burner now. I had him hook, line, and sinker. If he knew the whole story of my going to the biker bar and the arrest this morning, he might have hesitated, but he was on a need-to-know basis—he didn't need to know very much.

He said he would get back to me and I set a course out of the canal for Adams Key. The noise from the engine took over my thoughts for the next thirty minutes as I cruised up the bay. The biker was on ice and Justine would be at work until midnight. Martinez was going to figure out where the van was headed. I would give Grace the call, and get a few hours of sleep and a shower. Heading to Miami in my present zombie state was going to do no one any good.

I made it to the dock, and after the obligatory petting of Zero I went into the house and eyed the couch. But I realized it would have to wait when my phone vibrated. It was Martinez. He had located the van. The address was familiar, but I was not that intimate with Miami yet and had to enter it in the maps app on my phone. A red dot dropped in what looked like the same industrial complex that the biker bar was in. I texted Grace the address and went for the shower. I knew I'd never make it in time. The best I could hope for was that passing along the information would change my karma with Miami-Dade.

It was well past my time for coffee, but there was no other legal way I was going to get through the next few hours. The first sip restarted my brain and I realized I had made a mistake in giving Martinez the information so quickly. There were few chances to get on the positive side of the ledger with my boss. I should have known better than to throw him a bone like this without asking for something in return. There were probably better things I could get out of him: vacation time, overtime, or even radar for the boat. The list could go on. Living out here, I actually considered my life a vacation and overtime money had no sway over me as long as Jane, my ex, kept things the way they were. Radar would be nice, but what I really wanted was to stay on the case, and that meant he would need to change my status from furloughed to active. There were provisions for federal employees engaged in life safety activities to be exempt from the furloughs, and I expected a biker invasion of the park would fall into this category. I dialed his number.

"Got a team on the way," Martinez said.

"You know what you're walking into? Those bikers are heavily armed and have been drinking all day."

"SWAT will handle it."

I was about to ask about the investigation, but he cut me off.

"I'm calling this a life safety threat to the park. You're back in the saddle. Meet me in my office in thirty minutes." He disconnected.

I should have remembered my *Art of War*. Two thousand years ago, Sun Tzu had written: *"If you know the enemy and know yourself, you need not fear the result of a hundred battles. If you know yourself but not the enemy, for every victory gained you will also suffer a defeat. If you know neither the enemy nor yourself, you will succumb in every battle."*

If I had been thinking clearly, I would have known that in my current state I was clearly in the last category. Instead of being smart, I was counting on forward momentum to keep me going.

Now that I was back on the job I dressed in my uniform. Hoping to stay at Justine's tonight, I packed a backpack with enough clean clothes to replace the dirty ones stuffed to the side of my new drawer in her dresser. It was one thing to get the drawer; another step entirely for her to do my laundry. Just before I left, I called Grace and gave her the address Martinez had provided of the van's location.

The ride across the bay was uneventful, and I backed into my slip at the marina by headquarters. I noticed Susan's boat was back as I walked down the gangway to the sidewalk that led to the entrance.

The door was open and I glanced over at Mariposa's empty desk. Missing my only ally here, I walked upstairs and did a double-take when I reached the door to Martinez's office.

"Hi, Kurt," Susan McLeash said from her usual seat.

She was dressed in her too tight uniform and had a smug look on her face. Martinez cleared his throat.

"This is going to take more than you. Susan has been reinstated as a special agent. You two will be working together on this."

For the second time in an hour, the proverb from Sun Tzu hit me in the forehead. I hadn't thought at all about my enemy. Trying to keep the shock from my face, I turned to him. "When's the raid?" I was here for one thing and that was all he was going to get. I didn't need to ask the question; a glance across the desk revealed he was dressed in his podium uniform. Whatever happened had gone down already. I needed answers and wanted out of here. Martinez was probably grateful for the excuse to get back on the payroll and the face time with the media. Susan was in it for whatever she could get out of it. I wasn't sure what that was yet, but I'd have my eyes wide open.

"I've got some leads to run down," I said, rising from the chair.

"I'll expect a full report by tonight," Martinez said.

"Why don't you have Susan do it? She knows as much as I do." The words were out of my mouth before I could stop them. I knew I had to get out of there. Anything else that I said was sure to be used against me. I turned and left. Martinez's memory was very short when he had TV time.

Without looking like I was running away, I walked to the truck and hit the road. I kept one eye on the phone and the other on the traffic ahead as I drove west toward the Turnpike. Finally, when I turned onto the northbound entrance ramp, I relaxed. With the bust out of my hands, now I had to decide what to do about Pierce.

I had liked him immediately; probably my first mistake. There was no actual evidence of wrongdoing, but the indicators were pointing that way. Exhaustion started to take over again after the short-lived anger from my meeting with Martinez and Susan faded. By the time I reached the Don Shula Expressway my eyes were starting to close. I knew I was in no condition to tangle with Pierce. I stayed left and the minute I hit the Palmetto, I skidded to a stop. Rush hour brake lights were stacked in front of me. I was hoping a few kind words with Justine would get me an offer I couldn't refuse. Now I just hoped I could make it there.

If it was rush hour, I realized the news would be on as well. Living on the island had a few drawbacks. I wasn't a TV junkie—far from it—but there were some shows I watched and I liked sports. This had led me down the path of internet TV and I had several apps on my phone. Opening one that streamed the local channels, I switched between them until I found what I was looking for. Martinez was at a podium next to the Miami-Dade police commissioner and another man in a blue blazer, probably a Fed. They were all smiles, shaking hands and patting each other on the back. I knew it was just for the TV. The minute the red light on the camera went off, the knives would come out.

To the side of them was the contraband recovered from the arrest. I'd seen this show before. The evidence was placed for maximum exposure with baggies of white powder, shotguns, and ammo covering the table. In front were the same packing boxes I had seen being loaded into the van. I almost slammed into the car creeping in front of me when I took my one eye off the road and stared at the screen. There were only about half the amount of boxes I had seen sitting there. You could always count on the set being staged for maximum impact. In the past, I had seen empty boxes stacked to enhance the bust. What I was looking at was the opposite. Either they hadn't recovered all the drugs or someone on the inside had taken them.

The brake lights ahead started to blink and then went off intermittently as the traffic finally started moving. After exiting at the NW 36th Street exit, I made my way to the forensics lab. It was almost six and the lot was fuller than usual for this hour. Usually, the day shift techs made a beeline to whatever happy hour bar offered the best specials, but not tonight. I pulled into a space near the back of the lot and texted Justine that I was here. Since she had been forced to move upstairs into what she called the *big girl lab*, there were often other people around and we no longer had the same privacy as we did when she worked by herself downstairs. I think I would have been just as happy if she'd told me to go home as to come in.

She gave me the okay, and I got out of the truck. I felt more energetic now, but knew each time my nervous system was assaulted with another turn in the road, the highs were shorter and the crash deeper. I needed to find a bed soon.

The front door was still open, but the receptionist was gone for the day. I let myself in the security door with the visitors' code Justine had given me. Walking down the hallway, I reminisced about the old days, when I used to watch Justine swaying to her music for a few minutes through the glass partition in the hallway to her old office. There was still a glass partition, but it wasn't the same. Running floor to ceiling the smoked glass did little to dim down the glow of indicator lights from the equipment sitting on gleaming stainless steel tables. I entered through the glass door and found Justine bent over a machine near the back corner of the lab.

"Hey," I said.

"Hey back." She stayed focused on the computer display. "Maybe you should see this."

## 13

Trying not to let her warm body distract me, I looked over her shoulder at the oversize monitor. It might have made sense to her, but I stared at the screen not sure of what she was so excited about. "You're going to have to help me out here," I said. What I really wanted was to touch her, to hug her, and fall asleep next to her. I could see two of the day techs who were still at work glancing over at us. None of what I wanted was going to happen here.

"You're exhausted. Why don't you go back to my place."

"No; I mean yes, but go ahead and tell me what you're seeing."

"The guns are generic. We'll probably get some prints and maybe ballistics will come up with a match to a cold case. The drugs are cut seven ways to hell. There's acetone, sucrose, talcum powder, and baking soda. With all that crap, you might as well skip the dope and snort the rest. It'd have about the same effect."

This sounded common for street level drugs. The combination was actually pretty tame compared to what the meth heads out west used to cut their product. Rat poison, caffeine, and painkillers were all common there. Hunter Thompson's laundry list of drugs from *Fear and Loathing in Las Vegas* came back to me. The last line was memorable:

*There is nothing in the world more helpless and irresponsible and depraved than a man in the depths of an ether binge.*

I imagined the same applied to many of the items on the list of additives she called out. There was one at the bottom that I wasn't familiar with. "What's this?"

"There are traces of propionates. Probably the same chemical makeup that was found on the vest."

I still wasn't sure where she was going. I already guessed they were tied together; this just helped prove my theory.

She must have seen the look in my eye. "If I can isolate the propionate, I can find the source or at least what type it is." Her tone softened. "You really do need to get some sleep."

I wasn't going to disagree. As if I was a lost child, she ushered me out of the lab and walked me to the truck, making me swear I would go directly to her place and not wait up. There was no more kissing in the lab, but out here it was fair game. We embraced and held a long kiss for anyone watching. I got into the truck and realized that Grace was expecting me. I reached for my phone and called her.

"Can you hold him until tomorrow morning?" I asked.

"Yeah, I kind of figured you got tied up. Got a little surly earlier. There's supposed to be a lawyer coming, but we only have another few hours before we have to either formally charge or release him."

I made plans to meet her at eight in the morning at the county jail. That seemed to be the best time for interviews; after the prisoners had eaten and before the population was awake enough to become unruly. With more guilt than I should have felt, I headed to Justine's and was asleep as soon as my head hit the pillow.

With Justine's schedule, the blackout shades were required. She worked late, paddled early, and often napped in the early afternoon before starting all over again. They were enough to hold off the inevitable morning light, but weren't enough to keep out Martinez. I had forgotten to set an alarm, but as often as not, when I was on a case and stayed here, Martinez would call early.

I quickly shut off the ringer, rolled out of bed, and ran for the bathroom in an attempt to avoid waking Justine. Glancing over my shoulder to see if she was awake, I saw the bed was empty.

"Morning, Hunter," Martinez said. "Sleep well?"

He knew altogether too much about the minuscule details of my life. I held the phone away from my ear and saw it was after eight. "Got an interview in a few minutes."

"Didn't think it was a good idea to report the bikers' visit to Adams Key the other night?"

I wasn't only covering for myself now. I had to protect Ray, who probably should have reported the incident.

"I wasn't there."

"You might want to inform your neighbor that it is a violation of his contract not to report such events."

*Whatever* almost came out of my mouth, but I stopped myself. It sounded like we were going to get off with a warning.

"I have pictures. I'm working on enhancing them now, then I'll send them to your phone." Of course he had a camera on our dock. "I think one of them is being held at county."

"That's where I'm headed."

"Maybe you should take Susan. I want to make sure you understand I meant it when I said that she was working with you again. This shutdown has been hard on her."

Martinez and Susan had a different kind of employer / employee relationship. They'd never been caught doing anything, but the signs were all there. With the case opening up the park's payroll, he had included her so she could get a paycheck. It didn't take a special agent to figure out he favored her. Now, on top of everything else, I had to find something for her to do. "I'll text her some instructions."

"You do that. And that report you promised me?"

There had been no promise. "Yeah, I'll get on that." It seemed the appearance on the news from last night had already worn off. "I gotta go," I said, and disconnected. I sat on the edge of the empty bed. When I went to set the phone on the night table, I saw a notification. It was a text message from Sid. I was kind of surprised the night-time coroner was text savvy, but thanked him for not calling and waking me. The message said to call at four p.m. when he got in. At least I had some time.

It was eight-thirty by the time I reached the county jail. I would have liked a few minutes with a cup of coffee and a notepad to start to figure things out, and worried that with everything that had happened I would forget something. Maybe Martinez was right, and I should do a report.

Grace met me outside the interview room. Thankfully her partner was nowhere in sight. I apologized for being late. "It's all good," she said.

"Has he talked yet?"

"No."

"Why don't you give it a go? He knows who you are."

I entered the stark room and sat on the only piece of furniture that wasn't bolted down. Across from my seat was a table and single chair—this one didn't move. The man sitting across from me was covered in ink. I figured I could probably eliminate half my questions by studying it: what gang he belonged to, who his girlfriend was, where he grew up...even his football team was represented by a happy-looking dolphin with a helmet that didn't match anything else.

The one question that I couldn't answer was *why me*, so I asked it. "I'm special agent Hunter with the National Park Service." This was one of the rare situations where the title didn't sound lame. "What can I do for you?"

"I know who you are, dude."

I knew who he was, too, but wasn't ready to let him know. "Okay, and you are?"

"Grinder."

That too was tattooed around his neck. "What can I do for you?" I remembered the name from the other night.

He looked down at his hands. "I got some information, but I'm going to need a deal."

Of course he did, but I wasn't about to call the DA. "Why don't you answer my question first?"

"You were at the bar the other night. I saw you with that other dude."

I stared straight through him, trying to buy some time. If I played this right, I might find out why I had been set up and how Martinez had gotten the picture.

He was getting antsy. "I thought you guys had some code about ratting people out?" I asked. Maybe if I could figure out his motivation it would help.

"I'm already dead, just don't know by who yet."

"You still haven't answered why you asked for me." He looked at me like I was the dumbest guy in the room. Coming from a guy with an orange jumpsuit and shackles connecting all his moving parts, that wasn't much of a compliment.

"That dude you were with. I already told you. Now are you going to get the DA or what?"

"You told me it was him, but why? Answer that and I'll see what I can do."

He looked around like the walls had ears. They did of course, and eyes. With the threat of police brutality everywhere, it had become standard procedure to record these interviews. "He's a two-timer. Playing both sides, if you know what I mean. Dude's all tight with Doc and the board, but we all know he's a Fed."

So Grinder wasn't the only one walking on both sides of the street. "Give me a minute." I got up, went to the door, and knocked. Grace opened it for me. I could tell by the curious look on her face that she had been listening in.

"I can put him in protective custody for another twenty-four hours. That'll buy us some time."

"Should we talk to the DA's office?" I wasn't sure what procedure was for this kind of thing. My involvement usually ended with the arrest.

"Might as well get them in the loop, He's looking at time for the guns and drugs in the car. We've got a twenty-year bargaining chip."

"He's looking for a get out of jail free card."

"Aren't they all. Let's play it out," Grace said.

I went back inside the room. Grinder looked up at me with a cocky smile. He knew we'd play along—at least for a while. I'd been around criminals and interview rooms before. The contrast between the foolish actions that got them here and the craftiness to get out always amazed me. As dumb as he'd had to be to drive over the speed limit at four a.m. with the bass booming loud enough that the vibrations felt like an earthquake in the neighborhoods behind the twenty-foot-high concrete sound walls that lined the highway, and his back seat loaded with guns and drugs, Grinder was confident he would walk.

"Protective custody for twenty-four hours. I'm going to need more information on the club. President down through the delivery boy. I want names and titles." The last bit had come to me as I sat there. Tearing my pages of notes from the pad, I pushed the blank pages and pen toward him. Without another word, I got up and left.

"Good thinking, but your buddy Agent Pierce can probably do that for you," Grace said.

"I'm thinking Pierce fits in there somewhere." I wasn't sure if I should tell her my suspicions about the missing drugs and decided to keep that close for now.

"You're not going to like this, but my partner used to work for the FBI. There was some kind of disciplinary action and he was let go. There're all kinds of rumors, but he's pretty tight-lipped. Just before 2008 when everything crashed, the county was growing so fast that the department had a shortage of officers to open sub-stations in the new neighborhoods. There weren't a whole lot of questions asked, if you know what I mean."

That explained the chip on his shoulder. "You think he hates the Feds more than he hates me?"

She shrugged and I guessed there was only one way to find out. My phone vibrated and I glanced down at it. As if he had been listening, Ron Pierce's name flashed on the screen.

## 14

I let the call go to voicemail. There were some things I had to sort out before I talked to Pierce. He seemed to know more about my whereabouts than Martinez. His intel was most likely coming from Susan McLeash, but I had no proof. I didn't know if I could get it, either. With our history, confronting her was not going to get any answers.

I reconsidered talking to Dick Tracy. It's not a good thing for an investigator to allow his ego to dictate actions, and I knew this is what I was doing. "Maybe it would be a good idea to sit down with your partner."

"I think if you two could put your dicks away you might get somewhere."

She had pretty much nailed it. I offered to get Grace a cup of coffee while she called him. She declined and I remembered that she drank some concoction that required a barista. I wandered down the hall and got a cup of the local black.

"He's due in an hour."

At least he wasn't rushing in on my account. I looked at my watch, wondering if I could get anything done. Sitting here in my park service uniform at the county jail was an unsettling experience. Perps and arresting officers streamed by and I caught glances from both. For different reasons, both groups thought I was inferior.

I remembered Sid's message. "I'm going to run by the ME's office and see if the autopsy report is completed." I could at least take care of this bit of housekeeping. Autopsies were not my favorite pastime, and this seemed a clear-cut murder. It was customary but not required for homicide investigators to observe the procedure. And until this morning, I had been working on my own time and I'd thought that a good enough excuse to miss it.

"Okay. I've got some paperwork." Grace walked out through the security doors with me. "He's reaching out; don't leave him hanging."

So was I, but she had set up the meeting and I would respect that. I squinted and noticed the humidity as soon as we were out the door. It was hot. Not summer hot yet, but you could tell it was coming. We agreed to meet back at the station in an hour. I went to the truck and typed the medical examiners' office address into my phone. The map app calculated it was over a half hour drive from the metro-west detention center. There was not enough time; I put the visit on the back burner.

Looking at the map on my phone, I saw there was still a dot on the paint shop where Pierce kept the bikes. With nothing better to do, I decided on a quick drive-by. The more I could learn about Agent Pierce, the better.

When I pulled into the narrow street I noticed there was a lot more activity than there had been here two nights ago. Although the units had rollup doors, I could see now that most were businesses. The street was lined with work vans and trucks. I parked where I had the other night, out of sight of most of the units, and was about to get out of the truck and have a look around when I realized that I was in uniform.

A park service agent walking around and asking questions about an FBI agent wasn't the brightest idea. In the back seat was the backpack I had packed and forgotten to bring into Justine's last night. Reaching into it, I grabbed a T-shirt and swapped it out for my uniform shirt. The khaki shorts were nondescript and I got out feeling a little better about blending in.

Locking the truck, I pocketed the keys and started walking toward the closed door of Pierce's unit. The adjacent doors were open and I decided to have a look. The closer space looked like it belonged to a plumber. Racks of pipe and fittings cluttered the space. I heard a man inside talking gruffly on the phone to whom I guessed was a disgruntled customer. Turning away, I decided to try the unit on the other side. I guessed that if he treated his customers like this, I wasn't going to get any information out of him.

The space on the far side looked like a woodworker's shop. I could hear the sound of either a planer or router coming through the open door, where a fan blew sawdust into the air. I'd played around as a carpenter during the Northern California winters, remodeling our old farmhouse that, thanks to the cartel, was no longer in existence. If there was something I'd learned about carpenters it was that they like to talk.

I waited by the door until the machinery stopped and I called out a loud hello. A man came out carrying a stainless steel mug. He was ready to talk.

"Hey, my name's Kurt Hunter."

"Steve Brown." He extended his hand.

I looked at the man in front of me. His shaved head would have gleamed if not for the thin coating of sawdust. He had a goatee that stretched partly around his face. If he'd had tattoos, he would've looked more like a biker than Pierce.

"You know your neighbor?" I motioned toward the closed door.

"Sure. I know most of the guys on the block."

I listened as he talked. He tended to ramble and I had to refocus him several times. By the time he finished his coffee I had found out that there were two men that ran the paint shop next door. He was impressed with one and not so much with the other. I pegged Pierce for the other. They both seemed to be around more in the evening, not unusual for custom bike guys, as their clientele was mostly nocturnal. There was a woman that came by as well, and after his detailed description of her I thought it might be the one who had set me up for a picture in the club. After a long story about his wife not allowing him near the shop on weekends he realized he was out of coffee and said he had to get back to work.

I walked up and down the block of units and found no one else willing to talk. At the same time, I checked for surveillance cameras. Most had none and I figured the tenants cared more about their privacy than their protection. There was one discreetly placed above the paint shop. If he checked it, Pierce would know I had been here. To cover my tracks, I knocked loudly on the door and waited. I hadn't expected an answer and didn't get one. The office had a CLOSED sign in the window, and after peering through the glass door I could see it looked like it was seldom used. If his goal was to stay under the radar, Pierce had picked a good location. I went back to the truck and drove to the station hoping Tracy would shed some light on the mystery.

It turned out he had a bigger grudge against Pierce than he had with me. Making me feel like we were almost allies, he told me about the task force he and Pierce had been on. For three years, between 2005 and 2008, they had worked together. It wasn't surprising that it had been disbanded due to missing drugs. That seemed to be a theme here. Somehow Pierce had avoided scrutiny while the rest of the group had been fired. He finished with a bitter rant about the Feds having better pay and benefits than the county. Maybe that was his grudge against me. After my personal experience with the shutdown I wanted to differ but held my tongue. Slowly the façade disappeared and he was back to normal.

I had enough on Pierce to place him high on my list of suspects; he was actually the only one with a name. The bikers were guilty by association, and I tried to figure out where the smoking gun was. Pierce might have been involved with the missing drugs and his behavior was certainly suspicious, but the timeline I had constructed didn't have him near the scene when the man had been killed at the lighthouse—unless my timeline was wrong.

"Did you see the autopsy report on the guy at the lighthouse?"

"That was your baby. We got the drugs."

I should have known better than to blow off the autopsy. Homicide was the cause of death, but what I had missed were the details that wouldn't throw up a red flag with the coroner. Sid had obviously seen something.

I thanked Grace and her partner and we agreed to leave Grinder on ice. Then we would have to make a decision. That gave me the rest of the day to figure things out. My first step was to fill in the blanks in the coroner's report. Leaving the station, I went to the truck and headed over to the building behind Jackson Memorial Hospital that housed the medical examiner's office. I was more comfortable around Sid, the Jersey-bred, almost-retired, night-time coroner, but he worked the night shift. Instead I got his protégé, Vance.

After quickly changing back into my uniform shirt, I went inside. I shivered as I walked downstairs to the lab, thinking this was the coldest building in the city. The new crime lab looked futuristic compared to the more old-school décor of these examination rooms. The walls were covered with white subway tile, and the stainless steel had long ago lost its luster. The lighting was bright and white, making me almost squint when I entered.

Vance was off to the side, working at his standup desk. I cleared my throat to let him know I was here and he looked up. Though only a handful of years younger than me, he was from a different generation. The greased up hair and carefully groomed beard and mustache were all held in place with some kind of semi-lustrous gel not made to hide the fact that it was there. His lab coat showed a plaid shirt underneath and I would have bet his jeans were tighter than I would have deemed comfortable. I resisted the urge to look down at his socks that I could guess had some kind of design. Allie had accused me of wearing dad jeans, so maybe it was having kids that had separated us beyond our ages.

"Thought you'd be out fishing with the shutdown and all," he said.

"Back on the clock. The bosses up in the Ivory Tower declared this was life safety and put us back to work. Did you do the autopsy?"

"I stayed and worked on it with Sid last night. It appeared to be what you'd expect from what we saw at the scene."

I thought there might be a *but* coming that would justify my trip here. "Nothing unusual?"

"When they look this easy, they never are. Sid's from *Sopranos* country and he's seen it all. He found a few anomalies that I don't know if I would have caught. It turns out that the man wasn't killed at the lighthouse and the cause of death wasn't the knife wound."

I appreciated his honesty. That was the clue I'd been looking for, only it felt like it put me further from the truth. "How's that?"

"We sent some samples over to Justine and I want to wait for Sid to have another look before saying anything official."

Vance was the head medical examiner mostly because Sid had turned it down. The older man had more years of experience than Vance had been alive. Vance often deferred to him. "What time does he come in?"

"Should be here around three or four."

"Mind if I come back then?"

"That'd be good. I think he said something about a mafia killing several years ago in Jersey that was similar to this."

I thought it too bad that there wasn't a reference guide on gang-related killings. They were usually creative, but not original. An internet search might be in order and I thought about swinging by the crime lab, but the days of using the computer in the privacy of Justine's old lab were over. For once the clock was moving too slowly.

## 15

AT FIRST IT HAD LOOKED LIKE A CLEAR-CUT GANG RETRIBUTION KILLING. With the information that Vance had just shared, that the murder had been committed earlier and possibly at another location, the water was quite a bit muddier. I decided to revisit the scene of the crime. Sid and Justine were not due in to work for another few hours and I was still in "avoid Pierce" mode. We had originally assumed that the murder had been committed on the balcony where the body had been found. It was so well staged there seemed to have been no reason to look further, but now I wondered if there might be evidence we had overlooked. For once the shutdown might be working in my favor, as the lighthouse had probably been locked up since the crime scene techs had left the other day. Ordinarily, it was open whenever park personnel were on the island.

I left Justine a message and headed to Homestead. The midday ride back to headquarters was uneventful. I pulled into my parking space and when I saw both Martinez and Susan's vehicles there I tried to make an end-around the building and get to the dock before they noticed me. Martinez was ahead of me as usual and had made a rare trip from his desk to the dock. Susan McLeash was of course right behind him.

"Going somewhere, Hunter? What about those reports?" Martinez asked.

A boat blew by the entrance to the small park service marina at about twice the posted speed. I had noticed boaters flaunting the rules since Monday, when the shutdown began, and expected it to only get worse. The presence of the park service boats on the water was often enough to keep things under control. I don't think I'd written a speeding ticket since my first month in the park.

Martinez had desk legs and wavered as the wake rolled under the dock. He made a beeline to solid land, calling after me that Susan would be with me from now on. I put my hand to my ear as if I didn't hear him and turned to my boat. Susan was undeterred and followed.

"Where're we heading?"

"I'm heading to Boca Chita to have another look. You're free to come, but you better take your own boat. I don't know if I'm coming back here."

That didn't seem to bother her at all, and I relaxed as she started to untie her lines. The last thing I wanted was to be attached at the hip to Susan McLeash. Pulling out of the slip, I looked back and saw her just behind me. Tempting as it was to race her, I followed the posted speed past the boat ramp at Bayfront Park. It was probably a good thing for the boaters to see there was still a sheriff in town; with both park service boats heading out I suspected they would be more observant of the park rules. Somehow the fish, lobster, and crab here knew the boundaries better than the boaters and the populations thrived inside the park. The people tended to push those same boundaries, often claiming ignorance even when they had chartplotters that clearly showed their boat's position and the perimeter of the park.

Susan was tentative on the water. I knew she preferred a barstool to her boat, and I could almost hear her cursing me as I pulled away from her. It was satisfying, but in the end leaving her behind would serve no purpose. A mad Susan was a dangerous Susan. What I needed was to find something for her to do that would keep her occupied and out of my hair. Paperwork would fit that bill. As soon as we reached Boca Chita, I intended to dictate my report and email it to her to transcribe. Her name next to mine on the bottom would justify her paycheck, and that would be good enough for her.

With at least part of a plan in place, I slowed and let her ride the smooth water between my wake. Despite the quagmire I was in with the case, I soon found I had a smile on my face as the boat hopped over the low waves. I'd never been a boater in California. The coast and water there were unforgiving. The shore was rock strewn with seamounts, and the water was always cold. Mark Twain had been dead on when he'd said the coldest winter he had ever spent was a summer in San Francisco. I remembered taking Allie to the bay, and wearing our down coats in August.

Florida was a boater's paradise. It hadn't taken me long to become hooked on the feeling of freedom, similar to riding a motorcycle, but without the restriction of those bothersome lanes. When the boat went up on plane and the warm air blew through my hair, I couldn't help but forget everything else.

The feeling was short-lived. With the seas down, we reached the small harbor in about twenty minutes. With Susan on my tail, I slowed to an idle and entered the protected water.

I was surprised to see it full, with boats rafted two and in some cases three deep. Tying two boats to each other when the seawall was full was legal. Three was not, but I wasn't about to start writing tickets, especially when I saw the people aboard. I hadn't paid much attention to the boat traffic on the way out, and now, faced with an island full of bikers, I wondered where this was going.

I had heard about motorcycle club runs. They were made famous in the '50s by Marlin Brando in *The Wild Ones*. The Hell's Angels took things to a whole new level in the '60s, often invading unsuspecting towns for a weekend. It was a crafty sheriff who could navigate those waters without a riot. The tradition had continued, but most clubs were exactly that: motorcycle enthusiasts that enjoyed riding together, and the past incidents had faded into history. Their presence was often a boon to the locals, not a call to man the hospitals and clean out the jail cells.

The scene playing out in front of me was definitely the '60s version.

Drifting into the middle of the turning basin, I dropped fenders on both gunwales, not sure what my plan was. Susan pulled up alongside and I thought about anchoring one of the boats outside of the harbor so we would only have one to deal with. Before I could tell her, I saw a man waving his arms over his head and calling for me by name. He was dressed like a biker in blue jeans, a denim shirt, and a vest. I idled closer and recognized Ron Pierce. He directed me over to one of the boats, only rafted two deep by the lighthouse, where he hopped from the seawall and crossed to the outside boat to throw me a line.

It was my best and only option. Something needed to be done here and when I looked back toward Susan to coordinate our docking maneuver, I saw her on the phone. Her decisions were seldom good and I bumped my boat into reverse, cutting the engine toward her stern. Tapping her boat, I at least distracted her while she yelled at me. The ruse bought me a little time and we were soon tied off.

I thought about sending her out to ticket the boats that were three deep, but with the crowd gathering around the seawall, I decided against it. Though she would have gone into it blindly, knowing Martinez would be impressed with her production and the income he could add to his budget, I wouldn't put her in that position. I did recognize the opportunity to see how she and Pierce acted together.

She was savvy enough to realize that her beau was working undercover, but she still sidled up to him in her annoying post–fifty-year-old way. I had pegged Pierce for around forty and found it interesting how some menopause-aged women reacted when a younger man showed them some attention. But I had bigger things to deal with and now that I was on the clock, I could no longer be selective about how I did my job.

The island offered primitive camping, and ordinarily a ranger would be by to collect overnight fees. My concern was the general atmosphere and the safety of any other visitors, not whether they paid or not. I doubted there were any tourists left and hoped they'd managed to escape to the campground at Elliot Key. Alcohol was legal here, but it was a long way to the closest liquor store: seven miles by boat and another half-dozen by car. When the stock ran low out here, I suspected there would be some impaired boaters. That was something I needed to worry about and I asked Susan to have Martinez call in some backup.

She ignored me and continued to cozy up to Pierce. It was hard to tell if he was acting or if he really liked her. I had seen him looking at every woman he saw at Alabama Jack's yesterday and still had to figure out what his game with Susan was. In an odd way, I felt protective of her. Justine and I had saved her from several bad decisions already and I expected our work wasn't done.

Not wanting to put Pierce on the spot, I walked over to the lighthouse. Several bikers asked if I was going to open it up, and whether they believed me or not. I responded truthfully I had no key. That brought another problem to the table: I had come all the way out here to see if there was evidence the body had been dragged here and now I had no access to the crime scene.

Pierce came up next to me, apparently not caring that he'd be seen talking to the law. When I looked at him, I noticed a stark contrast between him and the rest of the bikers. His oil-stained, torn, and dirty clothes matched everyone else's. It was his eyes that were different. Most of he bikers had a dull look; his were alive. He looked like one of them, but at the same time stood apart—almost as if he was their lawyer or accountant. Apparently he had garnered enough of their respect and the group moved away when he got close. It could have looked to them like he was negotiating with me on their behalf.

"What are you guys doing here?" he asked in a whisper.

"Wanted to check something out," I said.

"Maybe this is not a good time." He raised his voice so the closest bikers could hear.

I wasn't sure what to do. Leaving would reinforce his standing in the group, but I didn't know if that was going to benefit my investigation. "How long are they going to be out here?"

"Hard to say. Usually when the beer runs out, it's time to go. It's kind of a wake. You'll probably have the place back in a few days."

I realized that the killer was probably somewhere in the crowd staring at us. Having a captive audience was both good and bad. I had to take a chance and hoped that if the order came from him, Susan wouldn't report it to Martinez.

"Get me into the lighthouse. I'll do my thing as quick as I can and leave you to your party."

"That can be arranged." He called a couple of men over and explained their mission.

They accepted and within a few minutes the lock was hanging loosely on the shackle. "Keep them away for a few minutes and I'll be out of your hair."

"If things were that easy..." he said.

I watched as a group started to line up and enter the lighthouse. My crime scene was quickly becoming defaced.

## 16

"Can you buy me a little time here?" I asked Pierce as I watched a dozen bikers enter the lighthouse, each carrying a case of beer. Several others filed in behind them, including several women. A minute later, I heard voices and then music coming from the small balcony where the body had been found. They were going to be a while.

At least that part of the crime scene had been thoroughly documented. It was the outside and the stairway leading up to it that I wanted to see.

"Let them sort it out themselves. Be patient and watch the survival of the fittest in action." Pierce stepped away and started talking to Susan.

Sitting on a low concrete wall across from the entrance, I watched as the lighthouse turned into a nightclub, including several bikers acting as bouncers. It was clearly members and old ladies only. Pierce was right. After about fifteen minutes the groups seemed to sort themselves out and no one else entered. I sat there for a while longer just to be sure. My gaze drifted away from the lighthouse to the campground, where tents and makeshift shade structures had been randomly set up in the normally organized clearing. It was hard not to notice some of the arrogant looks I caught from the group. They somehow knew that I felt powerless amongst them.

The group as a whole was a mixed bag, kind of twenty-first-century biker diversity. There was certainly money here, evident from the boats tied up in the harbor. The crafts ran the gamut from small skiffs to several that would have gone into six figures. From a quick count, I figured that there were at least eight bikers to each boat. This had been an organized invasion.

I moved toward Susan and Pierce. "May be a good idea to get some pictures of the harbor. I'd bet some of those boats have been liberated."

"If I could, agent," Pierce interrupted. "They see you taking pictures, the phone will be the least of your worries."

He was probably right. "I'm going to call Miami-Dade and see if they'll do a flyover."

"Your funeral. Right now you and Susan are tolerated because you are with me. I wouldn't do anything to change that."

Unfortunately the club didn't have an organizational chart posted on their website. He was right again, and I again wondered what his standing was. There was certainly a level of respect shown to him. I had no choice but to back off.

"I'm going to check out the lighthouse," I said, walking back to the boat to get my makeshift crime scene kit, which consisted of gloves and several evidence bags I had stashed in the console. After grabbing it, I headed to the entrance of the sixty-five-foot tower. A crowd started to gather around me as I worked. At first I felt threatened. It soon became apparent that they had no intention of interfering and understood I was trying to solve the murder of one of their own. There was no way to tell whether they would allow the justice system to punish the perpetrator or take it into their own hands, but for now, our priorities were the same. First we all needed to know who the killer was.

Thankfully Pierce had Susan's undivided attention, leaving me free to work on my own. If the murder had been committed off the island, there was only one likely avenue over which the body could have been carried to the balcony above us. The lighthouse was set on a narrow peninsula that formed the northern edge of the harbor. The water on the outside was too shallow for a boat to approach. Even if you were unfamiliar with the area, the visible propeller scars were an obvious indication to stay clear. That left the seawall inside the harbor. There was a small chance they had brought the body from the beach on the ocean side where I had watched the crabber the other day. But when I looked in that direction, I could see there was no way any evidence would have survived the mass of people milling around.

This time of year there were rarely more than a dozen boats out here at one time and they usually tied off near the far end of the seawall, which offered easier access to some of the more secluded campsites. Maybe there was a chance something had survived there. Walking along the concrete edge, I studied the scarred surface. I wasn't sure what I was looking for, because after a few days in the sun and salt, everything looked like rust stains. After finding nothing suspicious, I moved to the walkway, where I got down on my hands and knees and started crawling. I'd passed by this area a dozen times since the murder and hadn't noticed anything unusual. I caught some snarky comments from the crowd, but this was the only way to see anything.

About ten feet from the seawall I found my first clue. It was the opposite of what I had been looking for. Instead of a dark stain, what I saw was clean concrete; like it had been freshly etched.

Unless it is newly poured and sealed, concrete is seldom clean. It is a porous composite made up of aggregates and Portland cement. The cement by itself is brittle and needs the aggregate for strength. In most cases, on land, concrete is mixed at a plant and uses rock for the aggregate. Out on the islands, the concrete is often mixed with gas-driven mixers, using cement brought in bags and whatever the substrate is available locally, often dredged from the ocean floor. The material often includes brittle shells, which decay over time and leave voids and pits. What I was looking at was one of those voids. Something appeared to have accumulated in it, etching the surface.

I would have liked to ring the area with crime scene tape, but decided the nature of the outlaw was to break rules and the barrier would just taunt them—and I didn't have any. I stood and stretched, wondering what my next move should be. The crowd took this as an indication that I hadn't found anything and started to disperse. That was fine with me and I extended the moment until there were only a few people hanging around. I figured that once their beers were empty I would be left alone.

There was definitely something here; whether it had value as evidence or not was over my pay grade. I did know that it was fresh. Unless I had a jackhammer and could bring in the entire slab, I needed an expert and texted Justine with a vague "hey". There had been some repercussions that had trickled down to her from some of my other cases. With few resources of our own I was forced to rely on Miami-Dade's benevolence. I guess I had abused it.

While I waited for her to answer, I looked around at the few remaining spectators. A couple off to the side, drinking and making out under the shade of one of the few palms, caught my attention. It wasn't anything special they were doing, but they gave me an idea of what to do with Susan. The party had moved on at this point and I walked over to Pierce.

"What do you think about going undercover, Susan?"

I saw the smile on her face. If there was an opportunity for glory she was first in line. Her problem was she never evaluated the consequences of her actions.

"What do you have in mind, Hunter?" Pierce asked.

"I'm thinking a little makeover and Susan can be your old lady." The image at once disturbed and amused me. But if they went for it, Susan would be occupied and out of my hair.

"Yes!" she answered. "You good with that, baby?" She put an arm around Ron, who shrugged it off.

I still didn't know where he really stood with her, but she was a dog with a bone when she wanted something. Gauging her reaction, I had apparently opened a door to a fantasy of hers. Pierce was silent for too long and I started worrying that he was going to blow up my plan.

"I suppose if you guys are going to be hanging around, one of you might blend in."

"Oh, Ron," Susan crooned.

"Better get out of here, then, before they remember you."

"How am I going to get back?" she asked.

We spent a few minutes working out the details. Pierce had a boat tied up on the seawall acquired from an unknown source. From the twin outboards and narrow beam I guessed the go-fast boat had been confiscated and was now owned by the Feds. They arranged a rendezvous with the pretense of buying more beer. Smiling, Susan went to her boat, untied the lines and pushed off. She idled out of the harbor and we watched as she got up on plane and headed back to headquarters.

"What do you aim to get out of this?" Pierce asked.

"We've both got a dog in this fight. You have the gangs and drugs; I've got a murder. It doesn't take a parole officer to figure out that the murderer is probably out here. We need eyes and ears."

"Okay, as long as our lines stay clear."

I could have warned him that she was trouble, but something held me back—maybe the gut feeling that he was as dangerous as she was. They'd be perfect together. My phone vibrated and I moved to the seawall to take the call.

"Hey," Justine said.

"Hey back. You get a paddle in?"

"Pretty good. Got about eight miles. What's up?"

"I got something out here on Boca Chita." I explained what I had found. "What do I need to do to get you to look at it?"

"You're at Boca Chita now?"

"Yeah; quite the scene, too. The bikers have taken over the island."

"It's all over Facebook and the news is showing pictures. Pick me up at Dodge Island. I'll run it up the flagpole, but no one besides me would take this one."

She was right about that. Most techs were not like the badasses portrayed on *CSI: Wherever*. They were generally nerds and geeks. Justine was both of those but had an adventurous streak as well. I looked out at the water to estimate my time of arrival. "Give me forty minutes." There were no speed limits out here. Travel time was all about the weather.

"Deal. Give me five minutes. I'll clear it with the boss and text you back."

I went to the boat and took in the fenders on the outside that I had used for Susan's boat. Looking back at the island, I could see the party was still going on up on the balcony. The rest of the action had moved farther inland where there was more shade. Several boats came and went while I waited. The departures generally were one or two people leaving empty-handed. The arriving boats were crowded and packed with beer and food. This party was just getting going. A helicopter flew overhead, hovered, and came back around for another pass. I could see the local news station's logo on its side. The media attention would only add fuel to the fire.

The engine was already running in anticipation when Justine texted that we were a go. I released the lines and was quickly out of the harbor and heading toward Miami's skyline. I stayed inside the bay, and after passing between the #1 and #2 markers at the edge of the Featherbed Banks pushed the throttle up near its limit. Now that I was back on the clock, fuel was no longer an issue, and with nothing less than ten feet of water below my hull all the way back, I pushed the boat to its limit. Soon the seven remaining buildings that made up the outpost known as Stiltsville appeared on my right and I took a quick glance over. Before I could reminisce about the murder there, I was into the main channel and lined the bow up to the center span of the Rickenbacker Causeway.

Dodge Island lay ahead and five minutes later I pulled up to the giant tires secured to the seawall and used for bumpers. Justine was there waiting and I helped load her equipment; not failing to notice that she'd brought an overnight bag. When everything was aboard, she dropped down to the deck and gave me a quick peck on the cheek. I returned that with a real kiss, pulled away from the dock, and headed back to Boca Chita.

Encouraged by the news coverage and incubated by the beer being drunk as the sun passed through the sky, the island was loud and rowdy when we returned. As we'd arranged, Pierce's boat pulled in just after we docked. I nudged Justine to look back, wondering if she would recognize Susan. If she could, she was better than me, because what I saw was frightening.

## 17

"What have you done?" Justine asked.

The tone of her voice was my first hint that she didn't approve; then I realized she didn't recognize Pierce. "That's that FBI guy, Pierce." That didn't seem to faze her.

"So, you've let a sociopath loose at a biker convention. How do you think that's going to end?"

She had seen Susan in action and knew what she was capable of. "Pierce should be able to handle it."

She turned away, clearly thinking that I had made a mistake. I looked at the happy couple and accepted the fact that she was probably right. Susan was dressed for the event; almost as if she'd been prepared for it. With her hair curled and falling loosely around her face, she had the disheveled look down, but even from here I could tell it was held in place by a whole lot of product. Her makeup leaned heavily on mascara and eyeliner, with bright red lipstick setting off her china-white skin. It actually looked better than her usual pancake makeup. Her middle-aged breasts were propped up and revealed by a tight shirt and vest whose buttons strained at her midriff. Tight jeans finished the ensemble. I had to wonder if these had all come out of her wardrobe and if they did, where she hung out on weekends. Pierce handed her a bottle of beer and the two walked together into the crowd, looking very much like they belonged here. Even if her identity was discovered, what had gotten Susan suspended—illegally firing weapons, killing suspects, and coercing witnesses—would probably elevate her status with this group. I turned back to Justine and tried to change the subject. "Here's what I found."

"Lead on, but I still don't like this."

If I'd had a dead body, she might have been distracted enough to forget. There was little that turned my girl on like a fresh corpse. I hoped I had found something of consequence or her already skeptical mood was likely to turn against me. I grabbed one of her cases and led her to the area I had found.

Justine bent over and then went to her knees when she saw the etched concrete. This immediately drew a crowd of spectators. I had to think it was her butt they were commenting on rather than what she was doing. She was oblivious; focused only on the evidence.

"Why didn't you tape the area off?" she asked as she opened one of her cases. "This could have been ruined."

I breathed in relief. The scolding implied that I had found something of value. There was no good response, so I nodded and asked her what I could do to help.

"Grab the other case from the boat," she ordered.

Reluctantly, I left her for the few minutes it took to retrieve the case. When I returned the crowd had thickened and I could hear some of the comments. Justine was clearly a satisfactory addition to the party. Ignoring them I kneeled next to her, trying to shield her body from the crowd, and opened the case. I couldn't help but notice it was heavier than the other two, and when I opened it I found the answer. There were several hammers and chisels inside as well as enough wrenches and screwdrivers to take apart an engine.

"I thought about jackhammering it up," I said, trying to break the tension.

It was her turn to ignore me and I stayed quiet, handing her the tools as she asked for them. She had a ball peen hammer and a cold chisel ready to remove a section when she stopped short, leaned over, and looked like she was sniffing the concrete. "Come here and smell this," she ordered.

Catcalls answered when I leaned in and we touched heads. I wanted to look at her, but placed my nose against the concrete and breathed in. To my surprise there was fruity smell. "Smells like fruit."

"Correctamundo. I would guess whatever did this belongs to the propionate family. I'd have to do some testing to see which one, but that stuff keeps showing up."

As curious as I was, with the crowd around us, an explanation would wait. "What do we need to do?"

She stood and for the first time noticed the crowd gathered around us. "We should clear the scene and document the trail, then get some samples."

We both looked around, wondering how to accomplish this. Moving a crowd of bikers was easier said than done. Before I could figure out what to do, the loud base of a boom box started up and distracted the crowd. It was like someone had yelled *squirrel* and the group had moved on to the next shiny object. I was curious and watched where they were headed, only to find a woman dancing on a picnic table.

"Crap, that's Susan," Justine whispered.

I wanted to reply that at least she was doing something useful, but held that thought. "She likes her attention."

"Aren't you worried about her? I mean, I know she does some crazy stuff, but she's one of the good guys."

That was debatable. "Pierce has some standing here." I still didn't know how, what, or why. "He'll handle it. The area's clear here. Let's at least take advantage of the distraction."

"Just keep an eye over there. You're responsible for her."

I wanted to take her in my arms and kiss her right then. I couldn't ask for a better role model for Allie. I agreed and we switched to work mode. Justine, used to working alone, was efficient and I let her take the lead, doing whatever she asked and watching Susan at the same time. There were several women dancing now; I hoped there was safety in numbers.

We knew that the trail led to the lighthouse, making it easier to identify the path of the chemicals. Within a few minutes, Justine had yellow numbered cards placed along the route and was taking pictures. The trail did indeed lead to the entrance to the lighthouse and I tried not to get excited at the discovery. She was back at the spot I had originally found, sniffing around like a hound dog. Finally, she settled on an area and asked for the tool case.

She donned safety glasses, and placing the chisel about six inches away from the spot, she began to tap the blunt end with the hammer. She held the tool almost perpendicular to the surface and started tapping with the hammer. I let her go, not wanting to be a know-it-all, but she was getting nowhere. I was about to say something when I heard another bass booming louder than the one in the campground.

The music coming from the table Susan and her new friends had been dancing on stopped suddenly, and I looked over at the group. Someone called out and they ran to the beach. Watching them move reminded me of some of the schools of fish I had seen diving. Each movement by any single person echoed through the group. Fish schooled for protection; it was the opposite watching the herd on the beach. They were the predators.

Susan had been left behind and I took the opportunity to both see what the new distraction was and to talk to her without anyone seeing. Justine, still struggling to remove the sample, waved me away and I walked over to the picnic table.

"You might want to take it down a notch. It could go badly if these people find out who you are," I said.

"You think you know so much about everything. I'm just doing the undercover thing." She started dancing again, this time to a song coming from the water.

"Susan." I almost wanted to slap her and bring her back to reality. "Undercover means discreet."

"I got your discreet right here, Hunter." She banged her hip against me, reached over and grabbed a beer bottle, which she quickly drained.

I wanted to ask her how many she'd had, but the answer didn't really matter. After less than an hour as an undercover agent, Susan McLeash was drunk. Justine was right; this wasn't going to end well. A new song started playing, this one louder than the first, and Susan took off in the direction of the crowd. Running after her and dragging her back to headquarters crossed my mind, but that could backfire easily. The only thing I could hope for was that she had her phone. I would have to brief Martinez and ask him to call her back in. Hopefully, she would listen to him.

I moved closer to the group, staying far enough away to not attract attention, but I wanted to see what was happening. They were dancing, shouting, and calling lewd comments. Nothing unusual, but their energy was directed at the water. I moved to a clump of trees nearby that looked like a good vantage point as well as an offer of concealment.

Out on the water, less than a hundred feet off the beach, was a very expensive boat full of very expensive women. The name of a prominent strip club on South Beach, that I was all too familiar with from a prior murder case, was stenciled in bold letters on the hull. The girls, thinking the barrier of water offered protection, were posing and encouraging the men—and women—on the beach.

There were several other boats stopped nearby, though none as close. Apparently, the social media posts and news coverage were fueling a fire that was already dangerously close to being out of control. Several bikers, clutching several beer bottles between their fingers, were wading out to the boat, and I realized the predicament the boat and girls were in.

There was a hundred feet of water between them, but it was brown. If the group wading toward them were determined or drunk enough to make it through the muck, they could easily navigate the thigh deep water and reach them. From the looks of the two fresh white scars its propellers had plowed through the seagrass, the boat was going nowhere. Looking at the nearby mangroves I could tell the tide was starting to fall. They'd probably floated in and dropped anchor not realizing that the tide was their enemy.

From the look of the two men at the helm, who were drinking from insulated tumblers and laughing at the action, I doubted they realized the lower units and propellers were becoming engulfed in muck. There was a chance they could get free now, but with every passing minute their situation got worse. If I yelled, I could possibly attract their attention, but the crowd would likely turn on me. The only solution was to go around by boat.

Justine was alone, sweat dripping from her brow, still working the concrete, when I returned. Without telling her what was going on, I offered to help. At this point she was defeated and handed me the tools. I quickly looked at the concrete as if it was a living thing, studying the fissures and cracks for a weakness. I found a small crack and placed the chisel with the tip almost flat against the surface. Justine was about to say something, but I gave the chisel two light taps and she stopped when it started to disappear under the concrete. With a few more hits, a large piece came free.

"We have to go," I told her.

"What the hell? Are you some kind of concrete ninja?"

I handed her the tools and took the evidence bag from her. "It's spalling. The layers separate. It's because of the salt." I left the explanation at that and grabbed the case. We reached the boat and quickly loaded the cases.

"What's the rush?"

"You'll see in just a minute. Can you take us out of here and to the beach on the other side?"

I had no worries about her running the boat. After releasing us from the dock, I started pulling all the extra line I carried from the holds onto the deck while she worked the boat. By the time we reached the ocean side of the island, I had a bridle put together with two hundred-foot lines.

"Holy crap, this isn't good," she said as we rounded the point.

# 18

THE TIDE WAS RUNNING STRONG NOW AND I COULD FEEL THE PULL OF the water against the boat when we stopped to plan our approach. Ahead of us, a stream of bikers were in the water now, trying to make their way to the boat. The women aboard had become less flirtatious and I could see panic on some of their faces as the front-runners approached. If not for the muck, they would have easily crossed the twenty feet to the boat, but the quicksand like marl sucked them in with every step. The heavier men sank to mid-thigh, and several gave up and turned back. The two men at the helm finally recognized the danger; one went to pull the anchor, the other started the engines. We were close enough that I could clearly see there was no water coming from the exhaust port. If they continued to run them, the engines would overheat.

"Okay, Kimo sabe, what's the plan?" Justine asked.

"Tides running out. If we can get over to the sandy bottom, we can tow them into deeper water." What I didn't mention was that the boat would create a barrier between us and the bikers, who I didn't expect to be happy when the party ended.

Justine took a minute to gauge the current and idled to the boat. The men at the helm saw us and started to wave us off as if everything was okay. This might not have been a mayday, but it was in my jurisdiction and I was back on the clock. It was my decision, not theirs.

We were about two boat lengths away. "Shut down your engines!" I yelled across the water. The men appeared to panic and gunned the engines. A stream of dark brown silt appeared behind them as the propellers fought the muck. "You're going to burn them up."

They appeared undeterred and I wondered what they were protecting. "I don't care what you have; we just want to pull you out." The men talked amongst themselves. I saw them look at the approaching bikers, now only ten feet from the boat. Probably close enough to smell them. Finally, they realized the threat.

"Okay. What do you want us to do?"

I held up the VHF microphone and signaled six-eight with my fingers. A minute later they acknowledged on the radio. "We have to pull you backward." Towing them forward would only further entrench the engines. "Take the bridle and attach one end to each stern cleat." They looked confused, but there was no time for a Coast Guard Auxiliary boating course. "I'll come aboard."

Justine looked at me and I shrugged. Though she recognized the danger, she probably didn't like the idea of me aboard with a boatload of strippers. "Drop me on their bow." She idled toward the boat, slowly raising the tilt on our engine as we crossed onto the flat. Even with the engine raised to the point that it was barely sucking water, I still felt the drag of the bottom. With a final nudge, Justine got the boat within a few feet of their bow. "You got it?" I asked.

"Right on. Let's get this done."

With the lines in hand, I went to the bow of the center console and hopped across the water to the larger boat. The two hundred feet of line threw me off balance, and I landed awkwardly. Getting up, I moved quickly to the stern and separated the lines. With the bridle secure, I took the towline forward and tossed it across to Justine, who tied it off and returned to the helm. She could have used a hand to keep the line clear of the props, but managed to circle the stranded boat and slowly move to deeper water. The lines came taut and I felt a tug, which even though I'd been expecting it still threw me into the gunwale. The boat came free just as the first biker reached it. The girls were all huddled together by the cabin and I could see the relief on their faces when their boat slid into deeper water.

The boat started to move and the closest man grabbed the gunwale in defiance. I stood frozen watching his cold dark eyes as he held on. One arm came over and grasped the combing and I saw another man's arms land on the transom. "Start the engines!" I called. The man at the helm didn't hesitate. The second I heard the flywheels catch, I released the towlines.

I thought about slamming something against the men's grasping hands, but the force of the water running against the hull as we idled off the flat was enough. They both lost their grip and floated back to safety. The crowd on the beach had been silently watching until now. They surged into the water and I had a moment of panic until I realized they couldn't reach us. I looked for Susan, finally seeing her with Pierce, hanging on the edge of the crowd. There was no going back to the island for me; she would have to be my eyes and ears now.

A few minutes later, Justine had recovered the lines and pulled alongside us. The women gave a chorus of what I thought was heartfelt thanks, mixed with a few offers that I hoped Justine hadn't heard when I crossed to the center console. The entire time, the men had said nothing.

Before I had reached the helm of the center console, the boat was thrown hard to port by the wake of the go-fast boat as it sped away. Justine and I watched it climb up on plane and head back to Miami. The rest of the boats, their occupants bored now that the show was over, started to disperse as well.

"Well, cowboy, them cowgirls sure took a likin' to you," Justine said, punching me in the arm.

I was relieved that was over. "We should head back to your lab."

"I've got a better idea," she said, sliding away from the wheel.

I moved in to take her place and glanced back. She was pecking out a message on her phone and I wondered what I was in for now. A minute later she was back beside me.

"Where to?"

"Dodge Island. Sid will pick us up," she said.

I wondered what she had in mind and hoped it wasn't payback for missing the autopsy. I couldn't help but notice the strip club boat ahead. The women looked fully recovered now, and I couldn't help but watch until they turned into the Miami Beach Marina. Dodge island was to the left and I turned away. We passed the eastern tip, where the pilot's station was located, and followed the seawall until I spotted the Miami-Dade Coroner's van. Sid was standing beside it and stepped forward to help with the lines.

Justine and Sid were close in a father and daughter kind of way. She thrived on his mentoring and he loved the attention. There was a mutual respect that I wished I had with Martinez. I still had to break the news about Susan working undercover to him and had been composing an email in my head on the ride over.

We left the boat and I got into the back seat and braced myself for the ride. Sid climbed into the driver seat and assumed his position. Hunched over with the steering wheel almost touching his chest and his nose to the windshield, he started the van. I had seen this show before and reached for my seatbelt, pulling it tight around me. Thankfully he didn't have to back up and the van lunged forward when he jammed the transmission into drive and accelerated. There are not many times I am thankful for traffic, but this was one of them, and when I saw the cars lined up on the MacArthur Causeway, I relaxed. I could see Justine had also eased her grip on the handle mounted to the dashboard. It turned out we were both premature as he spun the wheel and accelerated onto the shoulder.

"Sid, what are you doing?" Justine yelled at him.

He pretended not to hear.

"Sid!"

"What are they gonna do, put me out to pasture? Might as well have some fun before I go."

I stayed quiet and kept my death grip on the door handle. Finally the traffic eased and gravel flew from the rear tires as he accelerated, cutting off two cars before we reentered the legal lane. When we reached the mainland, traffic resumed to normal, as did his driving. I was close to used to it by now. Tentatively I released the door handle and pulled out my phone. It had been several hours since I had checked it, and the screen was full of notifications.

Scrolling through it I saw two from Allie. The rest of the world could wait. The first was just a smiling face good morning. The second was an "OMG what are you doing?" Below the text was a picture of me on the boat with the strippers. Whenever there were scantily dressed women around, there were generally cameras, but after studying the picture for a minute, I realized it had been taken from the beach. From the angle the picture was taken from, it appeared to have come from curiously close to where I had last seen Susan McLeash.

To confirm my suspicions my phone vibrated and when I looked down at the screen, I saw it was Martinez. Hoping Sid would run off the road now, I answered.

"What the hell, Hunter?" he yelled.

I guess that was the new hello. I knew better than to interrupt him.

"I just got a full report from Susan. That picture'll make the freakin' news in a hot second. It's already all over social media."

I could tell he was running out of steam. "Did she tell you the whole story? If we didn't get that boat out of there you'd be looking at a shark attack from all the blood in the water."

"It's all appearances, don't you get that?" He paused. "Never mind. Just get me a report so I have some ammunition when the press starts asking questions."

Now that Susan was feeding him information, I gathered that my decision would go unquestioned. I'd put her in a bad position, but now she was my only source on the island. Putting my anger about the picture aside, I texted her for an update—I needed to keep her close.

I texted Allie back with a quick synopsis of the rescue, making sure to include Justine prominently. Just as I responded to the last message, my head slammed forward and hit the seat in front of me as the van came to an abrupt stop when we hit the concrete bumper in front of the Medical Examiner's office. My legs were shaky when I got out and I noticed Justine's were the same. We shared a look common to all survivors and followed Sid's hunched-over form as he swiped his card in the reader next to the door.

The sense of urgency from the ride over disappeared the minute we entered his office. He went to the coffee maker and started fussing with the controls of the imported machine that Vance had brought in. There were several mutters of "I just want a black coffee", and finally the machine complied and he came over to the table where Justine had laid out the piece of concrete.

I wondered why she had brought it here instead of to the lab until he hunched over and sniffed it.

"Ah, the sweet smell of death."

## 19

When things go well they tend to go slowly; when they fall apart it's like dominos cascading into each other. That's what I was feeling when Sid gave us his analysis. After a short lecture on the chemicals emitted by the body during the process of decomposition, he finally got to the point. The chemical that had etched the concrete was one of the death smells, and often present on a recently deceased corpse. Having it drip from the body on an obvious path to where the body had been found was a red flag.

Vance had done the right thing and taken the liver temperature at the scene. Time of death could be determined by a temperature probe stuck into the deceased's liver; it usually just took some simple math to figure out how long the victim had been dead. Subtract the probe's reading from 98.6 and do a simple calculation. It was the standard, but didn't seem to work with my cases. The first several bodies I'd had to work with had been in the eighty-plus degree water long enough for it to buffer the reading.

"A corpse is like a fish," Sid said, raising his eyes over his thick readers.

I knew better than to respond. Class was in session.

"You're not going to find a bonefish in cold water. They like it warm."

I nodded, wondering where he was going with this.

"Fish are cold blooded. They will assume the temperature of their environment. Fishing 101, right?"

"Right," I said. I had learned from pursuing trout out west that water temperature was everything. My impatience overcame me and I took a stab at it. "So the internal temperature of a dead body will be affected by its surroundings." I was sure I had it now. "The man was left hanging over the railing in the direct sun. With the concrete deck below and the iron rail, the heat coming off them would artificially raise the liver temperature."

"College boy, too," Sid said to Justine. "And he can fish."

"Thinks he can, anyway," she said, smiling at me.

He then embarked on another lecture, ending with his assumption that based on the formation of this, that, and several other things, the time of death was close to twenty-four hours prior to what we had thought. That was a huge window.

They were having a grand old time at my expense, but I was without a theory and that bothered me. I moved to the side to think while they chatted about one of their current cases. What I had originally thought was a gang-related retribution killing over a drug deal gone bad was now looking like it had been staged.

If the goal of the murderer was to set someone up, it had what retribution killings didn't. My four puzzle corners were back in play: means, motive, opportunity, and the trigger. At least I wasn't starting from zero. There was a real motive now and I had an assortment of unsavory characters and a suspicious FBI agent to look into.

"Can we identify the substance being dried on the concrete?" Justine and Sid gave each other a conspiratorial look and then both turned to me. I would have taken a phone call from Martinez right now. I looked down at my watch and saw it was after five. The day shift at the crime lab would be gone soon.

"Let's go, lover boy," Justine said, reading my mind.

"Curious to know when you identify it. It's a slow day, maybe I'll dive into the corpse and see if Vance missed anything," Sid said.

"Would you have seen anything out of place without having this evidence?" I looked over at Justine, who was bagging the piece of concrete. I knew Sid enjoyed mentoring Vance. The old man had spent decades picking apart dead bodies. He gave me the *of course I would have* look.

"Thanks." I started to leave. "Can you tell Vance the water is about eighty degrees—perfect for bonefish."

I knew, as twisted as it was, that he had a sense of humor. I wouldn't have prodded him otherwise, but to my relief, he laughed at the barb.

"One of these days, I'll take both you boys out and show you how to fish."

I thanked him and said good-bye, thinking that excursion might actually be fun. Justine gave him a hug and pecked him on the cheek before following me out of the exam room. We left the building and stood in the covered entry looking at the parking lot. We both laughed when we realized we had no vehicle.

"I'm not going back and asking him for a ride," I said, pulling out my phone and pressing the icon for the Uber app. "Where to?" She still had not said it was okay to go to the lab.

"I gotta eat. Can we go grab a bite and let the day shift clear out? Then we can see what we have."

"Works for me." The sun was heading down now and I realized I hadn't eaten since I left the house early this morning. Not knowing when we would return, she had hitched a ride with a cruiser to Dodge Island where I had picked her up earlier. We decided to get her car from the lab. While we waited for the Uber, I wondered how Susan was faring out on the island. Checking in could endanger her. I'd have to wait for her to call. Seeing her hammer the two beers earlier, I doubted that was going to happen. In the back of my mind I started working on a contingency plan to get her out of there.

A car rattled to a stop just ahead of us and I looked to the entrance to see if someone was waiting for a ride. When the driver lowered the passenger window and called my name with a heavy accent, I almost didn't answer. Justine smacked me. Her hunger was turning to "hanger". The ride would have to be fine. The easily identifiable scent of Febreze hit us hard when we climbed in and I could only wonder what the driver was trying to cover up.

He said something close enough to the lab for me to confirm that as our destination, and took off. The car rattled badly as we left the parking lot and I wondered if it would make it over the causeway. I placed odds at fifty-fifty and would have asked Justine for her wager if I didn't suspect the driver knew more English than he was letting on.

All in all, it was an uneventful trip, especially compared to the ride over with Sid. When the Uber pulled up next to Justine's car, I was out the door before he came to a complete stop. I wanted out of here. We hopped in and beat the Uber rust bucket out of the parking lot.

Fifteen minutes later, we sat at a corner table in a Cuban joint eating some kind of pork dish that I couldn't pronounce. I liked it, though. Cuba actually had a cuisine, something I missed after living with California Tex Mex for most of my years. We were quiet as we shoveled the food in our mouths.

The overhead fans brought the smell of café con leche to me and I looked over at a couple a few tables over. They seemed to be winding down their evening like normal people. I turned to Justine and smiled. Their lives might look good on the outside, but ours was good on the inside and I wouldn't trade it for anything. She kicked my shin under the table and gave me a sideways glance at the couple —she had seen it, too.

"To the lab, Bat Girl?"

"Roger that, Kimo sabe."

We paid and left the couple to their normal lives. Traffic should have been light leaving the beach this time of night, unless there was a Marlins, Heat, or Panthers game, in other words about every third night plus playoffs. Tonight was one of those nights, and the causeway was lit up with red lights in front of us. My anxiety started to build as I became impatient with the slow-moving traffic. I felt close to a breakthrough, but the lab seemed so elusive.

Finally, we passed the stadium and the traffic pattern flipped. Cars were backed up coming toward us and we had a clear path onto the Palmetto. Pulling up at the lab, I looked at Justine and awkwardly asked permission to come in. Back in the day—a month ago—she'd had the old lab to herself. Things had been easier before the techs had to swipe their card to log hours onto the equipment they used.

Before she answered, I started pecking at my phone.

"What are you so busy with?"

"Sending a work order for the lab work." The hammer had come down from somewhere in the county bureaucracy about her not working on evidence without a case number or authorization. Grace Herrera had helped me out before when our cases overlapped, but this was a park matter.

"Right on." She laughed and punched me. "You can come in then and supervise your work order."

That was her signal that everything was good. I hit SEND and heard the swoosh that it was gone. Martinez was CC'd. I had to do it and was counting on him not seeing it until the morning. I got out of the car before she changed her mind and followed her into the building. We had to pause at the door while she swiped her card and, after a few seconds of anxiety, the buzzer sounded and we were inside.

It was almost seven and the lab was a dull glow of LED indicator lights. A brighter light was on by a workstation off to the side, but otherwise it looked like we had the place to ourselves. Justine went right to a machine, then went to the vault to get the evidence. I had no idea what it was and thought it would have been nice if they put ID cards with descriptions in front of each piece like in a museum. I stayed quiet; asking questions would only distract her.

After donning gloves and a mask, she took the piece of concrete out of the baggie with a pair of tweezers and gently set the sample down on a piece of glass in the center of the instrument. She closed the lid and pressed a button.

"Should just take a minute."

Before I could ask what the thing was and how it worked, the display on an adjacent computer monitor lit up. We moved to the workstation and read it. She was quiet for a minute, as if digesting the answer to our question and before she said anything, she changed programs and started typing. I assumed she was entering the results until a worried look came over her face. She was about to say something when my phone vibrated.

A text came through from Allie to call, which I did.

"Dad, that woman you work with is on the news."

## 20

I pulled up the local channel on my phone and thought about how it wasn't right for a fifteen-year-old to have seen and experienced what she had at such an early age.

"Can we go see them? Maybe this weekend?" she asked.

Her request was denied. Saying no to your kids is hard. They are often unrelenting and you have to hold the line. The first time a no turns into a yes, they will never forget. I remembered when it felt like that was the only word that came out of my mouth for days. We said good night and disconnected.

I sat quietly, thinking about the boats hanging around the island, while Justine ran another test. With the weekend coming up, if the shutdown continued, something would need to be done before this party turned into a spectator sport. The lab had several monitors, constantly streaming the news, and I turned to the closest. They were showing footage of the island shot from a helicopter. It was from earlier today when we'd been out there. I saw the camera zoom in on Susan, dancing on the table. I breathed in relief that I had already seen what Allie was referring to.

"I think I have it pinned down," Justine said, waiting until she had my attention. "Propyl propionate."

I gave her the *this means nothing to me look*.

"It's a chemical released by the body when it decomposes. I had a feeling from the pineapple smell."

"So, it could have come from the body when it was moved to the lighthouse?"

"Yes and no."

I was too tired for another puzzle.

"There should just have been traces. Not enough to leave a trail. Curious, though, it's also a paint solvent used for automotive paints. Do those guys have a garage or shop?"

I wasn't sure about them, but Ron Pierce did, and I recalled the paint equipment on the workbench. "Is it something we can compare to another sample if we find it?"

"If it was bought commercially there would be slight differences in the chemical composition. Companies will do that to obtain patents. It's a lot of work though and could take a while."

I got the hint. Unless the result of those man-hours was going to solve the case, the request would likely be denied. "We need to get into Pierce's garage." It sounded so simple when I said it, but getting a search warrant for a property probably leased by an undercover federal agent was easier said than done. Miami-Dade bore a grudge against him, but they were bulls in a china shop. I would have to go this alone.

I happened to glance over at the TV again. With the Capitol building as a backdrop, a drop-dead gorgeous reporter was interviewing what I guessed was a congressman. The closed caption stream running across the bottom of the screen confirmed I was right. It also said there was nothing on the table amicable to both parties. The shutdown would continue, leaving me two problems: the murder and the bikers out at the island.

I wondered if Pierce and Susan were still out at Boca Chita, or if he'd had enough sense to get out of there before it became a drunken brawl. Hoping she was sober enough to play along I texted her a concerned "hello", like it was coming from a friend.

"What'cha doing?" Justine asked.

"Texting Susan. I want to see if Pierce is still out there." I explained my theory about his garage.

She knew Susan as well as I did. At first she had been skeptical, but Susan had proven herself to be a loose cannon over time. "You sure that's a good idea?"

"I wrote it like I was a concerned friend thinking she was missing. As long as my contact information doesn't say 'special agent Hunter', she should be okay if someone sees it." Before I could think of how she had entered me in her phone, it pinged. "Got her."

"That's not always a good thing."

"SUP?" I entered.

"Party on. Wanna bring out some beer?"

I studied the message for a minute, as if there was a hidden meaning in her response, and decided it was what it was. "Can your friend run you back in for some?" I wanted to know where Pierce was.

"He's over in some big pow wow. Been there a while." Her tone changed. "It's dark and dirty out here."

I guess I had found her threshold, but there was no way I was going to come get her. Showing up in the harbor in a park service boat at this time of night to pick up a biker chick was not a good idea. Something else did occur to me. "Maybe Ray can come out in the morning?" The facilities would certainly need to be serviced and Ray hadn't been out there since the invasion. "I'll get back to you."

It was late, but I texted Ray anyway. I knew his procedure for work calls, especially when it was Martinez on the line—voicemail. If he didn't want to be bothered the phone would be off. They also had the benefit of Becky's phone for personal things. Though I didn't want to carry around two phones, I thought that might be a good idea for me as well.

Justine was over at a computer monitor now and after texting Ray, I went and stood by her side. She rubbed back when I pushed my body against hers. Her curves distracted me for a hot second until I caught a glimpse of the screen. She had already identified the manufacturer of the chemical. If it was commercially available the murder had occurred at another time and place. It was as ingenious a murder weapon as any I had heard of. If we hadn't found the trail in the concrete its occurrence in the corpse would have been ignored as a natural occurrence.

One of the addresses popped out. It was Pierce's garage. "Hey, that's the paint shop."

"How's that gonna go for you?" she asked with a mischievous look on her face.

"Well, there're two ways in." I threw it out there. She ignored the illegal route.

"Your buddy Grace is working the swing shift this week. I saw her last night. There's always a judge on call."

"Dick Tracy would love to get his hands on Pierce. Maybe it's worth a shot." I picked up my phone and texted Grace. While I waited for an answer, I checked my messages, not surprised that there hadn't been a response from Ray. My phone rang and I saw Grace's name on the screen. Deciding it was better to include Justine, I pressed the speaker button and placed the phone next to the keyboard.

"Evening, Agent Hunter."

I breathed out, hoping Justine hadn't caught it. There was friction between the two women. It was clear there was a professional respect, but there was something simmering below the surface. I brought her up to date about finding the chemical trail at Boca Chita and the delivery to Pierce's shop.

"Could be a coincidence," she said.

"Could be." I needed her to decide for herself.

"Or not."

"He's playing undercover biker dude out on the island. There's not going to be a better time." The line went quiet for a minute. She had access to the judge on call. There were a limited number available after hours to sign warrants, but unless the searches proved fruitful, you were burning expensive capital with them.

"Okay, type it up and I'll find a judge. You better be clear that it's an FBI agent involved. That's not something we want to come out later if this turns out to be nothing."

I knew it hurt our chances of getting a warrant, but she was right.

"I'll email it to you in a few," I said, disconnecting and turning to Justine. She relinquished her seat and I logged onto the super secret park service portal. After finding the form, I thought it more and more likely with every keystroke that a judge would sign it. There was also an odds-on chance that the FBI would be notified and Pierce would find out. I closed the window before I finished.

"No go?" Justine asked.

"I think I'm going to have a look myself first."

"You can't break in."

"No, just a look. Maybe there's something in the trash?" It was a shot in the dark but all I had. I texted Grace back that I had decided to wait until the morning. The relief was evident in her response. Having a fruitless search on a warrant issued during business hours was a whole lot better for your reputation. I told her I would contact her tomorrow and disconnected.

I got up to leave and started to say good-bye to Justine. "You going to walk?"

I hung my head. My truck was at headquarters.

"You know, having an ace crime scene tech with you might prove helpful."

I knew Justine was always ready for adventure. We had found ourselves together in some interesting situations in other cases and she had handled herself well; in one case even saving my life. "I didn't want to ask." It was the truth, at least. Putting her in harm's way was not always my choice, and not something I would ask of her.

"Glad I did, then," she said, closing the computer screen. She went to her desk and grabbed a case. "Could be some evidence. Ready?"

We left the lab and headed out to her car. During the otherwise quiet ride I gave her directions to the alley where the shop was located. We parked a block away behind a dumpster and started to walk toward Pierce's shop.

"At least I'm not seeing any security cameras," she said.

"I think the people in here want their privacy. Pierce has some covering his unit, though." The alley was sparsely lit. The shadows made it seem like there might be danger around every corner and I felt Justine brush up against me. We stayed close as we approached the roll-up door. To my surprise a light shone from underneath the worn weather stripping.

"What now?"

We had to make this look casual and I did the only thing that I could think of: I knocked on the steel door. I heard something move inside and jumped back when the door started to roll up. Worn boots were the first thing I saw, and as the door opened I could also see oil-stained jeans. Several seconds later the vest and finally the head of the man were revealed.

"Pierce here?" I asked.

"Little late for a visit?" He eyed my uniform.

"I was getting worried. Haven't heard from him in a while."

"He's hanging out on that island."

I moved forward slightly, but he mirrored my move, blocking the entrance. There was a faint smell coming from the shop, maybe paint. We were so close and I struggled to find a way in.

"You have a bathroom I can use?" Justine asked.

That broke the tension and I silently thanked her. The man stepped aside and motioned to the back corner where I had changed the other night. "Kurt Hunter," I introduced myself. I figured Pierce would get a full report anyway and could confirm my identity from the cameras.

"Bolo," the man said, again shuffling to the side to deny me entrance.

The door to the bathroom closed. He might not let me in, but if I could distract him for a few minutes, maybe Justine could spot something. I looked over at the Indian bike I had seen the other night.

"That your Indian?"

His look changed. "You know bikes?"

"Made in Gilroy, California. That looks like one from the seventies. My old man had one."

His body language changed. I took a chance and moved toward the bike. This time he didn't stop me. "Mind?"

"No, have a look." He moved to the side.

I went to the bike and knelt down to examine the engine. He leaned over and started to explain the modifications he had made. I'm not a gearhead, but at least I was familiar enough with the engine to know what he was talking about. When you find someone who is passionate about something it is usually easy to put them at ease and draw them out. From the corner of my eye, I could see the bathroom door open and Justine enter the workshop. She must have seen what I was doing and moved toward a storage rack loaded with chemicals.

I asked every question I could think of until finally I felt Justine by my side. From her look, I knew she had found something.

## 21

There was no need to tell him that I worked for the park service; I was in uniform. I assumed he and Pierce were business partners, but I had no idea if he knew that Pierce led a double life. I had gotten more than I had hoped for and thanked him for his time. Pierce would know I had been here from the camera pointed at the door. I had tried to scan the shop space for others and not seen any. That didn't mean they were not there and I hoped there was no video of Justine checking out the chemicals. Otherwise it would look like an innocent visit—unless you were a crooked FBI agent.

We walked quickly through the dark alley and were quiet until we reached the car. Once we had pulled through the alley and onto the main street, I was about to burst. "Did you find anything?"

Justine held up her phone. "Bingo. That's the stuff." I glanced at picture of the bottle she had taken while trying to keep one eye on the road. The bottle was about the size of a pint of alcohol.

"So, for the custom work they do, it could be normal?" I asked.

"That'd be over my pay grade. We went looking for it and found it." She put her head down and started searching for something on her phone while I drove us back to her apartment.

Originally, I had been excited to find the chemical there, but now as Justine rattled off the specs from a website she was looking at, it didn't seem all that unusual for it to be in a custom paint shop, and I started second-guessing myself. Negative thoughts are never good, and I realized how tired I was. I also knew how my brain worked and if I left it alone and got some sleep some of this might make sense in the morning.

"I don't know if I'm beating the wrong bushes here," I said as we pulled into her parking spot. It sounded a lot like whining because it was.

"How about a glass of wine and we'll recap."

I really wanted something with a little more punch, like the Appleton 21 rum that Mariposa let her husband have when guests were over. We walked up the two flights of stairs to her apartment and I stood back while Justine opened the door. I trudged over to the couch and waited while she opened a bottle of red. Sometimes, out of nowhere, things hit me in the head like a roundhouse punch; others take small jabs to get my attention. When Justine handed me the glass it was like a haymaker hitting a glass jaw.

"I'm sorry," I started. It struck me that me and my bad attitude were sitting on her couch sucking down her wine. It didn't stop me, though, and I finished the first glass in two gulps.

"What for?"

"I'll be better about stuff." We had come too far over the past year for me to screw it up with work. I was sitting here with a girl that had and would do anything for me, and my daughter. I had wanted to tell her I loved her for a while and rehearsed the words in my head while she refilled my glass.

"You want to talk about it or go to bed?" she asked.

I had an image of saying the words and having her fall into my arms. I would sweep her up and take her to bed and the world would be right. Unfortunately I think I dreamt it because I felt a tug on my shirt and realized I had fallen asleep. Slowly I got up and dragged myself to her bed swearing that tomorrow I would start paying less attention to work and more to what mattered.

Martinez didn't get that memo, and per his usual had gotten my location through my phone and was ready with a wake-up call. I grabbed the phone off the nightstand and swept my foot across the bed. Justine was gone. I was starting the day with no balls and two strikes.

"What happened to my report?" Martinez was wide-awake and on his game. It had been two days since the news coverage of the drug bust and the news cycle in his head was telling him he needed more. "Susan filed hers."

I almost blurted out something I would regret. "I'll be there in an hour," I said and disconnected. I got out of bed and peeked behind Justine's blackout shades. The sky was an ominous grey laced with shades of charcoal and the palm fronds were moving. I looked up at the Australian pines, whose tips reached high into the sky, and saw them swaying back and forth. Like a pilot could tell wind speed and direction from looking at a windsock, the pines told me the seas would be kicking up from the east. It would be a wet run until I reached the shelter of the barrier islands.

After dressing and drinking the cup of coffee Justine had left for me, I pulled out my phone and paused before my finger hit the Uber app. Shaking my head like I deserved what I got, I pressed it. After leaving Justine a note, I went downstairs and waited in her empty parking space for the ride.

I was relieved when the car pulled up with all its parts intact, and the ride to Dodge Island was uneventful. The boat was as I'd left it as well, and I hopped aboard with the forward line in hand. The tide kicked the bow out and I started the engine and released the stern. Minutes later, I was away from the pier and moving south. I steered behind Fisher Island to sneak a look at the water outside Government Cut. Even from a half-mile away, I could easily make out the small bumps on the horizon that would turn into four-foot seas. Choosing the slower inside route, I cut back behind the island to stay in the lee of Virginia Key and Key Biscayne.

There were some short exposed areas, but I was more or less dry when I passed Cape Florida and hit open water. It all hit then; the charcoal clouds that had been laced through the grey sky had come together and formed a solid dark line. Whitecaps were breaking over the shoals at Stiltsville, taking some of the punch out of the seas, but soon I hit the long exposed section leading up to Boca Chita Key. I felt the first drops of water and reached into the console for my slicker. At first I had felt strange wearing rain gear in the eighty-plus-degree weather here. Out west, the summers were dry and clear. When we did get precipitation it was usually during the winter months and you were already dressed for it. It had surprised me at first, but after scoffing the idea several times, I learned that even with the warm rain and mild temperatures you could still get cold.

The rain started beating down harder and I pressed down on the throttle after several cracks of thunder sounded close enough by to rattle whatever the seas weren't already jarring loose on the boat. I hoped Justine had made it in before the storm. She had said she wanted to ride some bumps and I could only imagine what the waves that were slamming against the center console could do to a lightweight paddleboard. Her race board was fourteen feet long, but was like a large toothpick.

I gritted my teeth and took my punishment. At least having to steer every wave forced me to concentrate on the seas ahead and not on my shambles of a case. I could soon see the lighthouse in the distance and decided to check out the harbor. It was an excuse to get out of the weather and update my report. When I got close enough to see the line of boats streaming out of the harbor, I looked up at the skies. Whatever the higher power was that kept our planet spinning, be it physics or God, it had more power than the U.S. Congress.

The bikers were leaving en masse and I decided to wait until the traffic slowed before entering. If they were going on their own, there was no point in antagonizing them. After twenty minutes or so, I watched the last of the stragglers leave and started toward the entrance.

There were still several boats scattered along the seawall; about a dozen by my quick count. They might have been the smarter ones, because as soon as I tied off to the seawall the storm seemed to break and the skies cleared. Two more boats had departed while I was securing the center console and I could see several more making preparations. The few that remained were some of the nicer boats with cabins that had provided shelter for the occupants. They also likely were more experienced boaters and knew how quickly this could blow over. I gazed out past the harbor mouth. The seas had already subsided.

Martinez might be waiting, but I'm sure he knew where I was by the tracker in the boat and on my phone. I could easily explain the detour as park business, which it was, in a way. My main goal was to make sure Susan wasn't still out here. I had set her up for this; it was the least I could do.

I walked past the small area I had chipped the concrete from. Martinez would be happy there would be no repair necessary as it looked like several other areas that had suffered some minor spalling. Our timing had been good. Twenty-four hours later and the evidence would have been washed away.

It only took a few minutes to walk the rest of the island. Abandoned tents and debris were scattered around the clearings and blown into the mangroves. It would take a few trips to haul off the trash, but there looked to be no lasting damage. In a week there would be no sign this had ever happened.

I took some quick pictures for Martinez that would hopefully justify putting Ray back on the payroll to clean up the mess. He would probably have downloaded them from the Cloud by the time I got there. Heading back to the boat I saw the last of the bikers leave and a strange quiet settled onto the island.

The sun had started to appear intermittently and I hopped aboard. Martinez had already been waiting an hour. I was closer to home than headquarters and I thought about going back to Adams Key. I could file a report from there. I was tired. The fishing would probably be off today after the storm passed, but the couch might be okay for a couple of hours. The lack of sleep had worn me down mentally from the case. I needed a break.

There was no way Martinez was going to leave me alone without a face to face, so I resigned myself to a trip to the mainland. The only thing in my favor was the following seas, that made the ride back easy. The waves were coming down fast and I expected they would be calm by the time I had to make the run back to Adams Key.

Half an hour later, I was tied up at the dock and walking into the building. The doors were open, but Mariposa's desk was vacant. There was a handwritten sign to go upstairs for help. That struck me as odd. The only public interactions that Martinez ever had were held in front of a camera. Helping wayward tourists or answering questions about the park were not ordinarily something he would be interested in. With the learning center and museum next door closed, there were only a few people milling around.

I could only shrug as I answered questions about why the shutdown affected the tours when they were paying customers. I did the best I could and headed upstairs. Martinez's door was ajar and I knocked before walking in. I heard him respond and I pushed the door open, only to find Susan sitting there.

## 22

Susan McLeash sat there looking like the Queen of Smug. She looked clean and rested, making me wonder when, and how, she had gotten off the island. The party had taken its toll, though. Her uniform looked tighter and her makeup was thicker. She had also adopted the heavy eyeliner and mascara look the younger women wore. It looked marginal on them and ridiculous on her. She flipped her hair and said hello.

"Sit down, Hunter," Martinez ordered.

I would have preferred to stand, making for an easier getaway, but his gaze directed me to the chair. I sat at an angle, facing away from Susan. Once I was seated, he pushed a file folder across the desk and sat back with one eye on his monitors and one on me.

"Take a look, Agent Hunter."

I opened the folder and pulled out the contents. Three typed pages were stapled together.

"We call that a report."

I started reading and braced myself for his rant.

"Somehow Susan found the time to write that up and have it on my desk this morning..."

He continued, but I let his words pass through me while I read.

The party was well documented and several key players were identified. There was no mention of the grounded boat or anything of real substance. I glanced back over it and realized most of the information could have come from the media coverage or the internet. I could tell by the smile on Martinez's face that he was happy with her. There was no need to look at her to know she felt her undercover work had been a success. I also knew better than to criticize her work. As badly as I wanted to know what her relationship with Pierce was all about I kept my mouth shut.

"Storm took care of the party." I pulled up the pictures and pushed the phone toward him. He glanced at me and moved the mouse on his desk. The screensaver disappeared showing my pictures on one of his monitors. He had already pulled them off the Cloud. It was like I was looking at someone else's work, and that's the way he was treating it. I guess once something made it to the Cloud there was no credit given. "I've been working on some other evidence." I almost said *real evidence*, but cut myself short. "Seems the body found hanging from the railing was staged."

"Really," Martinez said, turning away from the monitors.

I had his attention. "There is a chemical trail from the seawall to the lighthouse. We identified it as propyl propionate."

"'We'?" Susan asked.

I let it go and continued. "The chemical naturally occurs in decomposing bodies. It is also a highly flammable solvent. Traces were also found on the burnt vest." I could see I had his attention now and delivered the clincher. "There were small amounts in the heroin we found. If enough were ingested, it could be the murder weapon as well." I knew that was almost too simple a solution, but the facts fit. "Someone used the chemical to kill the man, knowing it would be passed over as the cause of death, then used the same stuff to start the fire. " I sat back thinking that was as much of a report as he was going to get.

Martinez appeared impressed. He smelt something bigger than just the murder at the lighthouse. "Are you close to finding where the man was killed?"

I had no intention of telling him about Justine and my sortie last night. Any mention of Pierce—good or bad—would have Susan running to tell her boyfriend what had happened the minute I left. She would probably give him a three-page typed report as well. If she performed as expected, I had an idea of how to use her for damage control. "There's also Agent Pierce."

"What about him," Susan said, sitting forward.

"He's working both sides of this."

"I can vouch for him," she said.

"Why don't you continue to work with him, then."

Martinez placed his hands on his temples. I had him on his heels now, and had to close the deal. I looked straight at him. "He trusts her. The bikers know who I am. They've pretty much accepted Susan's cover." He put his hands on the desk and sat straighter. I could see from the look on his face that his wants conflicted with his needs; he wanted Susan safe, and he also wanted her reinstated. The assignment made sense. Before he could answer she stood.

"I'll do it."

Martinez sat back in acceptance. At least I knew who the boss was now.

"Keep me posted, both of you," he said, turning back to the three monitors he had lined up on his desk. The third and largest had been added when Susan had been reassigned. I wondered if he would need to return it now that she was apparently—at least temporarily—reinstated.

Several people were at the top of the stairs when I left his office. They looked like a lost family. "Can I help you folks?"

"We were looking for the tours," the woman said.

"Sorry, folks, the facilities and tours are all closed due to the government shutdown."

They accepted my reply like sheep and started down the stairs. I stepped back to Martinez's doorway and caught his eye.

"Something else, Agent Hunter?"

"I was thinking that with both of us out working the case and Susan undercover, maybe it would be a good idea to bring Mariposa back. She can help coordinate the investigation and direct traffic from downstairs."

"We could use the help," he said like it was his idea. " I'll call her in."

Whatever worked was fine with me. Mariposa would be a big help in deflecting the tourists' questions. She would also be my eyes and ears here. With Susan McLeash running with Pierce, it was going to be essential that someone knew what was going on.

I left the building thinking I had done pretty well, then heard the sound of a truck pulling out of the parking lot. I didn't need to turn around to know it was Susan. She had wasted no time taking the bait. Now, I needed to be patient and let her reach Pierce. He would surely know by now that Justine and I had visited the shop last night. There was nothing I could do until she reached him. Walking to the dock, I saw no sign of the previous storms. If my mind were only as calm as the water, I might be able to make sense of things and thought that maybe throwing a few flies would help.

Fishing gave me a different kind of focus, one that often got my brain into a different place. There was something about stalking fish or game that put my senses on high alert. I could be sitting in the same spot with or without a rod and have two totally different experiences. With a pole in my hand, I saw everything, even things not readily apparent. It took a different kind of concentration to spot the signs, like the small, almost invisible humps in the water when a school of fish moved. That was the kind of focus I needed now.

I pulled out of the marina and into the channel leading to the bay. It was quiet; the post-storm period when everyone who had been out earlier was back in, and those thinking about it after seeing the improving weather weren't here yet. I would have liked to find Chico and scanned the parking lot at Bayfront Park for his truck. He was one of the guides that had helped rather than avoided me. I did my best with the local guides, knowing that with Susan usually spending most of her time behind her desk I was the only one patrolling the entire park. The guides knew and saw everything that went on here.

Passing the ramp, I headed out of the channel, and after passing the last marker I set a course for a small cove to the south of Adams Key. I had fished it on this tide before with good luck. If the storm hadn't shut down the fishing, I hoped for some small tarpon or maybe a bonefish. If it had, I would be content to throw some flies.

The ride across the smooth water cleared my head and I was soon pulling into the empty cove. The Power-Pole secured the boat and I reached into the console for the rod case. I knew better than to keep spinning rods aboard, but the four-piece fly rod fit into a two-foot long cylindrical tube that stashed nicely beside the extra dock lines and fenders. With the rod in hand, I pulled the small fly box and reel from the case and looked out over the water, trying to decide which fly to use.

I went with a chartreuse Clouser minnow, a multi-purpose fly. I'd started using loop knots recently to enhance the flies' action and it took me three tries to get it right before I was ready to make my first cast. Stripping line onto the deck, I wound up and with a sidearm motion dictated by the T-top, started false casting. I settled into a groove and was soon casting and retrieving without thinking about it. This was when the juices flowed, but a hit on the fly pulled me back to reality. Using my left hand, I put a little pressure on the line already between my fingers, and slowly raised the rod tip. At the same time I reeled with my right hand to get all the excess line lying at my feet onto the reel.

The pull increased and I held the line tighter, forcing the fish to pull it free. I sensed the head shake and lifted the rod tip again to set the hook. The tarpon cleared the water in the first of what would be several jumps and I leaned forward to give just enough slack that he wouldn't break off. I had all the line on the reel now and after releasing my left hand I was able to use the drag to fight the fish.

We went back and forth until I was finally able to turn the tarpon's head for the last time. Defeated, he came quickly to the boat where I grabbed the leader, bent over, and clasped the thick jaw. Holding the fish into the current, I released the hook and after a minute let go. With a kick of its powerful tail, it was back in the safety of the mangroves.

My heart was beating fast as I started stripping line again. After several casts, I was back in the groove and with the extra adrenaline from the tarpon my brain started to click. In this state of mind, I was able to climb above the fray and look at everything that had happened from afar. I soon realized that I was too close to things and my emotions were caught up in the case. As I swung the line back and forth, waiting for the perfect moment to release it, I thought I saw a connection.

Everything revolved around Pierce. Even before I had first seen him with Susan, he seemed to have had advance notice of both my and the bikers' actions. I guessed that could be what made him a successful agent, but there was something else.

I was so deep in thought that I almost missed the shadow in front of me. Through the clear water I could see the bonefish clearly as it followed the fly. It was unusual behavior for the skittish fish. It usually took a perfect cast and presentation to entice the elusive trophy to bite. I started getting excited, but as soon as it saw the boat, it turned away.

As I pulled the fly from the water and started the motion for the next cast, I saw the missing link. Instead of stripping the line in and readying it for the next cast, I used the reel. It was time for another kind of fishing. I put away the rod, used the saltwater wash down to clean the boat, and headed back to headquarters.

## 23

EVERYTHING PIERCE HAD DONE HAD BEEN CAREFULLY CRAFTED TO MAKE me look the other way. I thought back on our initial meeting, when he'd shown up on the police boat like he had been waiting for it, on the setup in the bar where my picture was taken, his relationship with Susan McLeash, and the party out on the island. The only thing that had thrown a wrench in the works was the bust that Stallworth had made.

By setting up the murder scene and subsequent wake / party on Boca Chita, he had used the government shutdown to his advantage. Not only did he focus my eyes on the island, he had carefully crafted a scenario to place all his competitors in one place—away from something else. Susan had looked well rested this morning, leading me to believe that she and Pierce had left the island shortly after I had yesterday. The storm might have given me another gift. By getting the bikers back to the real world, it might have forced the timeline on whatever he had planned.

The water ahead was glassy calm, allowing a light touch on the wheel and for me to focus on my idea. The more I thought about it the more comfortable I became with the theory that Pierce had set up an elaborate diversion. The question was how to prove that he'd committed the murder and what he was covering up. It had to be big if it was worth killing over, and by the time I reached my slip at headquarters and secured the boat, I had a good idea where to start.

I walked past the headquarters building and saw Mariposa's car parked in her usual space. Martinez hadn't wasted any time bringing her back. I would have liked to stop in and say hello, but didn't want to risk seeing my boss. My new theory required a fresh look at the evidence from the traffic stop, and I would much rather see Justine than Martinez.

Before heading out, I thought about texting Justine that I was heading her way, but stopped after a quick *hey*. She had been reprimanded for helping me before and I didn't want to put her in that position again. I decided instead to call Stallworth. He had made the arrest and would know what to do.

Unfortunately that turned into another decision—one I hoped I wouldn't regret. After explaining that the Highway Patrol's mandate was enforcement and not investigation, he suggested I contact the Florida Department of Law Enforcement. The FDLE could certainly handle the investigation, but I was leery of involving anyone new in the case. Instead, I chose the devil I knew and called Grace. I didn't want to deal with her partner, but at least this time we had a common goal and I knew she was a straight shooter.

She answered her phone and I explained my theory and what I needed. I could feel the tension over the phone.

"I'll give you anything that happens outside of the park. I just want him for the murder." That seemed to lighten things up.

"Give me a few minutes. I have to kick this upstairs and get approval."

I thanked her and disconnected, thinking I had better start a public relations campaign with the county before I was totally shut out. However, it appeared that the potential upside of the case had been determined to be greater than the liability of working with me. She called back and asked to meet her at the lab.

It felt awkward being there without Justine. I knew a few of the techs by name, but had never worked with any of them. Grace walked in and I breathed a sigh of relief when I saw she was alone. I let her take the lead and we were soon ushered to a large table and asked to wait while the evidence was brought out. I heard the swoosh of the vacuum seal break when the tech opened the doors to the Vault.

A few minutes later the tech rolled a cart toward us and we stood staring at the toolboxes Stallworth and I had found in the van. We donned gloves and stared at them for another minute.

"Where do you want to start?" Grace asked.

"If it were me…"

I heard him and turned. Dick Tracy stood behind me. My new BFF pulled on some gloves and worked his way between Grace and me. "It all depends what you're looking for."

I already knew that most of the toolboxes contained weapons and had mentally separated them. "What's the deal with ammo here?" I asked. I already knew that each state had its own regulations, with California leading the pack.

Instead of answering, he pulled out his phone, pressed a few keys, and handed it to me. The PDF showed the ammo that had been deemed illegal in Florida—quite a long list.

"Armor piercing is always hot, but they're around and cheap. Mostly Mexican loads and not generally reliable. The hot stuff are the shotgun shells. Flechette's and Dragon's Breath in particular."

I had noticed that most of the weapons were shotguns. They were all one offs, as if they were for display—or demonstrations. I remembered the shots fired from the crabber. "That's got to be it. Pierce is too smart to smuggle guns. They're too big."

He was skeptical. "There's money in the ammo. They might run four to six bucks a round where you can buy them, but as soon as you cross the state line, they're about four times that. It's not a get-rich-quick scheme, but you can make some serious coin without having to deal with the cartels and other importers. You can buy the damned things off the shelf in some states. Even though sale and possession are illegal in Florida, crossing the state line makes it a federal case, something the FBI would be involved in."

"Someone like Ron Pierce," I said. Dick nodded and I realized that having a common enemy might be a good thing for our relationship.

"Still seems like small beans for a guy with his ego."

I had to agree with his assessment, but every indication led me to believe Pierce had something to do with the ammo. We started opening and setting aside boxes. The firearms we put to the side. With all the boxes open we took a closer look at the ones with the shells. The rounds were neatly packed in foam dividers. I took one out and examined it. It appeared to be a standard 12 gauge shell with a brass charge and plastic casing. There was no outward indication of what the rounds contained, but there were three colors. This wasn't unusual for shotgun shells, which were not only classified by caliber but also contents. The size of the pellets, from birdshot to buckshot, were all identified by the color of the plastic casing. As we continued to sort through the evidence, there was still something bothering me, but before I could put my finger on it, I heard a voice behind me.

"Hey, kids."

I turned back and saw Justine. She came to my side and I couldn't help but notice how she kept some space between her and Tracy. "Hey. I think we figured out what Pierce is up to."

"And look at you two, playing nicely together."

I looked around when she said it and noticed that Grace was not there. It was interesting that Justine hadn't asked where she was. "I think he's bringing in illegal shotgun shells."

I could tell by the look on her face that she wasn't convinced and I thought about what had been bothering me. It was the volume.

"Let's go shoot some of these bad boys and see what we've got," Tracy said.

"How about we act like grown ups? Why don't you bring a sample over to my station and I'll tell you what you have," Justine said.

Tracy put his head down and helped me carry an assortment of the shells to her workstation. Starting with the yellow casings she clamped the brass primer in a small vice, then started to cut around the plastic casing. Small darts fell out.

"Flechettes," Justine said. She did the same to a round covered in the green casing and found the ingredients of a Dragon's Breath. When she got to the red casings, we both stepped back when a white powder fell out.

I jumped back. My first thought was Anthrax, but neither Tracy nor Justine even flinched.

"Y'all thought you had it all figured out. That would have worked nicely at the range. How about you guys leave this with me for a bit?"

"They're not shells?" Grace walked up behind us.

Justine had just placed a shell on a small digital scale. "Three ounces. Take one off for the charge and that's a whole lot of drugs in a small package."

The layers were piling up and I wondered what Pierce was really into. The drugs did solve my volume problem. Instead of each shell being worth twenty-five dollars on the black market, the drug-filled casings were closer to twenty-five hundred each. At twenty-five shells per box that was over sixty grand in a neat legal package—and that was wholesale. Using Martinez's math, the reported worth they called *street value* would be ten times that.

"I thought you said those guys were firing Dragon's Breath and Flechettes off the crabber the other day," Grace said.

"A double decoy. He gets the club to move the drugs thinking they're just illegal shotgun shells, which some probably were." I remembered the missing boxes from the load at Alabama Jacks. "The bust the other day. I thought there were missing boxes. They must have been the drugs. We were all proud that we had the illegal shells, but Pierce has the drugs." I did a little more math. "At twenty boxes per case, that's a million and a quarter wholesale dollars—and I counted ten."

"Let's see what we have here," Justine said, taking another red shell and emptying the contents into a glass dish. She placed them in a machine and a few minutes later the results came up. "Some pretty pure stuff."

Justine started to log the test results into the computer and prepare the next sample. Grace, her partner, and I stood there wondering what to do while she worked.

"I got this," she said, moving past us to the table with the weapons cache. It was clear that she wanted us out of her hair.

I followed her. "See you later?"

"Sure thing. Just get rid of Wonder Woman and her sidekick."

We made tentative plans for dinner. Seeing Grace behind her, she dodged my kiss and said a sterile good-bye.

"What now, Ranger Rick?"

At least he was asking my opinion and so I ignored the barb. "Good question. Maybe it's time to go see some of Pierce's friends and let them know what he's up to."

## 24

WE DROVE TOGETHER TO THE BIKER BAR PIERCE AND I HAD VISITED A few nights ago. When we pulled up I couldn't help but notice the long row of bikes parked in a neat line in front of the bar. The spaces didn't have placards reserving them, but I saw Doc's bike in the first spot. The rest of the lot was about half full, but Grace parked the unmarked car down a side street. "Unmarked car" was an oxymoron, as the telltale signs it was a police vehicle were there to see. The antennas, which barely fit in before cell phones, now stood out. Anyone taking more than a cursory glance at the vehicle would see the poor job of hiding the lights in the grill, and the metal divider between the front and back seats was a dead giveaway. It said Miami-Dade Police all over it.

"How do you want to play this?" Grace asked.

"We can't go in. They'll make me right away." I looked over at Grace and Tracy in their cheap business suits. They said "cop" all over them.

"What did you get out of Grinder?" I had forgotten all about our informant. Martinez had decided that Miami-Dade could handle the interview alone. Neither Grace nor Tracy had mentioned it, so I suspected it had gone nowhere.

"These guys don't rat," Tracy said. "He came up with a story and some names that we already knew."

"Maybe we ought to be the rats and tell them they've been played," I said.

"That's a dangerous move," Grace said.

We left it unsettled, which is not a very good state of affairs when you're in enemy territory. After a few minutes of disagreement, we made a plan, deciding that splitting up was the only way to cover the egresses. We each took our positions. Grace would stay out of sight by the bikes. Tracy took the far driveway and I walked around back to cover the rear. We had each other's cell phone numbers favorited, allowing us to make contact with one click. That was for emergencies. Texting was to be our main mode of communication, making voice calls unnecessary in all but an emergency.

Once we were in position, we exchanged messages and settled in to wait. The problem was we weren't sure what we were waiting for, but if there was going to be action, this was the likely place. After the murder and then the bust of Grinder and his partner, they would need to decide some things. There was no one left on the island and I hoped that the rest of the leadership were here.

For the first hour Grace and Tracy saw the only action and texted when someone they recognized entered or exited. I didn't know if it was a good or bad thing that there was no sign of Susan or Pierce. I was occupied by the steady stream of people in and out of the back door. It appeared the legal smoking area was out front; the weed was smoked back here.

It wasn't surprising that there was little in the way of security lights in back, making it hard to distinguish faces. From my spot behind a dumpster, I struggled with the stench of stale beer and worse while I tried to eavesdrop on their conversations as the bikers came and went. Most of the talk was about the success of the wake out on the island and how they had gotten the best of the Feds. Apparently the news that Grinder had been arrested had not been broadcast.

For the next hour or so it was more of the same, until my phone vibrated with a text from Grace saying that Susan and Pierce had just pulled up and entered the bar. I started getting anxious and thought about moving, but stayed put. We were here to watch and learn, and if we didn't stay in position we were likely to miss something. I had to trust them. A few minutes later, Tracy chimed in that several of the other leaders had arrived. My apprehension increased.

It looked like there was going to be a high level meeting and with Susan inside, I was expecting the worst. My heart almost went through my chest when the back door opened and someone was tossed out. Relieved it wasn't Susan, I watched as two men followed, delivering several hard kicks before spitting on him. The few smokers in the area ran for the open door and I peered around the dumpster at the man lying on the ground.

I heard him groan and suspected he had been hurt. He tried to rise and went down. Thinking this could be our break, I texted Grace and Tracy. Several minutes later, though I couldn't see them, they confirmed they were in position and had a visual on the man. It was my turn now, and I left the cover of the dumpster.

I had a gut feeling there would be no one else coming out for a while and went toward the man. Knowing Grace and Tracy were watching with their weapons ready gave me some reassurance, but with the door only feet away, I wondered if they could help in time if I were spotted.

"Let me help you," I said, extending a hand to the man. He didn't resist. Anything to get him out of here before they decided on a worse punishment would be to his benefit.

"Who are you?" he asked.

His voice was coarse, as if they had tried to strangle him. I dodged the question and grabbed him under the arm. He flinched from the pain and allowed me to move him to the edge of the parking lot. Just as I set him down, Tracy came running to our position.

I was out of breath from moving the man and Tracy took charge. "You have a weapon?"

The man reached into his boot and pulled out a knife, which he handed to me.

"Frisk him," Tracy said.

I reached over and gave him a quick pat-down, then nodded to Tracy, who lowered his pistol.

"Y'all gotta help me," the man whispered. "They're gonna kill me."

"We gotta get out of here before they come looking for him," I said to Tracy.

"Grace'll be here in a second."

Just as he said it, the unmarked car pulled into the back lot. Tracy stood and motioned her over. Together he and I placed the man in the back seat. I hopped in next to him, and before Tracy had the door closed Grace pulled out of the lot.

The car went quiet for a few minutes while Grace found a place she could pull over. She settled on a well lit park with several baseball diamonds and parked behind one of the dugouts. Several cars were parked nearby and I could see a few men tossing balls to a group of kids. There were also a few of the ever-present dog walkers. Her decision was a good one and I could see the man visibly relax when he saw the lights and people around and realized there would be no police beat-down. The downside of our being in the park was that if the bikers decided to come after us, innocents would be at risk.

"Talk," Tracy said.

All eyes were on the man.

"There's a drop scheduled. It's not usually my job to keep the inventory and shipments straight. The guy that usually does it was the one that got killed. I started to get it ready and that dude comes in with two cases he says to include. I know what's supposed to be going down, so I opened the boxes and found some red shells." He paused to clear his throat. "They had drugs. Man, we try and stay clear of that. Just the ammo, you know. All that comes in yellow and green casings, so I opened one of the red ones and found it full of heroin."

I wasn't sure how he had determined what drug it was, and figured the shipping and receiving manager for a motorcycle club probably knew more about these things than I did. It didn't really matter, though.

"I went and told the bosses, but that dude, he got all jiggy and went off on me. Said I was setting him up or something. Man, he talks like a lawyer and spun the whole thing nine ways to hell that it was my fault. What am I going to do?"

Grace turned to her partner and said something I couldn't hear. "We'll bring you in on some bogus charge and get you in protective custody until we figure this out."

The man looked relieved.

"You know when and where the drop is?" I asked.

"No, man; they tossed me out before they laid it out. Been using this old crabber for the ammo, though."

Somehow we needed to find the drop. They might believe him for now, but guilty or innocent, Pierce was exposed, and that meant Susan could be in danger.

"If he doesn't know where the drop is going to be, we are still nowhere," I said. We were talking like the man groaning next to me didn't exist.

"You said maybe we ought to tell them there's a rat on the inside. Maybe let them flesh out that rotten SOB themselves," Tracy said, directing Grace to go back to the bar.

The man groaned louder until he realized that we weren't going to sacrifice him.

We pulled up to the door. "You and me, Ranger," Tracy said, getting out of the car.

"You sure this is a good idea?"

He didn't answer, leaving me no choice but to follow him. As we entered, I could only hope he had a plan. He flashed his badge at the man working the door and we walked right up to the bar. The air-conditioning was working hard, but the place stunk of beer and sweat. There were some other scents in the air, which I chose to ignore. I motioned to the bartender and Tracy asked if Doc was here.

"Who's asking?"

There was no point in playing games. They knew who we were. Tracy moved closer to the man and lifted his shirt. The badge caught the light as did the stock of his pistol. He dropped the tail back down to cover them and waited. Instantly the entire bar was quiet. Several men made for the door; others hid in the shadows. It was an uneasy situation, but they had more to lose by messing with us. They knew their best route was to get us out of here, and that meant some degree of cooperation.

"Give me a minute."

The bartender swung up the access door and went to the back of the bar. I watched him knock on a door. He waited outside for a minute until it opened just enough for him to talk. A minute later, Doc walked out with a large man beside him. The crowd parted as they came toward the bar.

"Can I help y'all?" the larger man spoke.

"Just want a few words with Doc here."

"And you are?"

I almost asked if he was Doc's attorney, but held my tongue and reached into my pocket for my credentials. I stopped when he reached behind his back. "Kurt Hunter, Special Agent for the National Park Service."

"What? We left the island. You got a bill for the cleanup or something?" he laughed.

"We're looking into the murder. Just want a few words with your boss."

I guessed the vetting process was over when Doc nodded at him and he stepped back a few feet. He was out of earshot, but ready to spring into action if Doc was threatened. When the time came to make an arrest, we would need to find another venue.

Doc motioned us to a table by the bar and we sat. The activity in the bar ceased and all eyes were on us. Tracy nodded at me to begin.

"We arrested several of your members. Shotguns and illegal shells were confiscated." I left the drugs out to gauge his reaction.

"It was a routine traffic stop. Illegal search. The bust is bogus. It'll be tossed."

I wasn't going to debate the facts. "Seems like there was more to it than the shells." I watched his face.

"You trying to set me up?" He started to rise.

"Sit," Tracy said. "We don't care about the ammo."

He sat back down and seemed to relax. His reaction and body language told me that the club was in the ammo business. I didn't think he knew anything about the drugs.

Tracy swung from bad cop to good so quickly it confirmed my diagnosis that he was bipolar. "Just wanted to give you a heads-up that someone's using you."

This wasn't Doc's first rodeo. "You going to tell me why you're really here?"

Before any of us could speak, the office door opened and Pierce walked out. He knew we were here and I guessed that he had been watching us on the security cameras. I held my breath and waited to see if Susan was behind him. Just as I thought he was alone, he reached back to hold the door open before the automatic closer shut it and there was Susan McLeash.

I had to admit she could at least dress the part of an old lady. Her usual heavy makeup and tight clothes fit right in here. Pierce said something to her and she went to the bar, hiked up her embarrassingly short skirt, and slid onto a stool. Her back was to us, but I could see her face in the mirror behind the bar. I looked away when I saw her staring right at me.

Pierce saw us, and walked over as if he were the undercover agent he might actually be. If he were innocent, and knowing that he had infiltrated the club, our presence here could be putting him and Susan in danger. He pulled out a chair and sat down.

"You were saying?" Doc asked.

He was looking right at me and I hoped he hadn't noticed my interest in Susan or Pierce. I cursed myself for not having contacted her before we came here. I had let my distrust for her cloud my judgment. I looked over at Tracy and caught his eye. With Pierce sitting here we were not going to get anything out of Doc. It was time to go before something bad happened.

This little meeting had gone as far sideways as I was going to let it. I stood. "Thanks for your help. We'll be in touch." It sounded stupid, but he was preoccupied and I don't think he heard me. Tracy did, and gave me a *you've got to be kidding* look.

I glanced over at Susan's reflection in the mirror on my way out the door. Her head was down and she was typing into her phone. I had no doubt I would get a message from Martinez any second. We moved quickly once we cleared the door and didn't slow down until we reached the car. I had hoped for more of a tactical retreat, but figured that the bikers were more concerned about their internal issues than they were about us. We had planted a seed, now we needed to see if it would grow.

## 25

After another discussion, we decided to keep an eye on the place, hoping Pierce would panic. Sitting across the street under a burnt-out streetlamp, we waited. The man next to me had apparently passed out. I elbowed him to make sure he was still alive and got a grunt in return before he collapsed against the opposite door. No one left the bar for quite some time and I had to guess there was a meeting going on. I could only hope it would have the intended result.

Finally the door opened and a group of men appeared. They had the alert look of men ready for action. Several carried what looked like heavy bags, which they put in their saddlebags. Behind them were Pierce and Susan. I could almost see the grin on her face as she climbed on the back of Pierce's bike. Watching Tracy and I leave the bar with no results was a *shadenfreuder* moment for her: the guilty pleasure derived from someone else's misfortune—mine. I glanced over at Pierce, who was putting a similar bag into his saddlebag. The look on his face was one of concern.

While we waited for the men to mount up, my phone vibrated. It was Martinez, and I could sense the panic in his words. Watching the two dots on his screen must have been driving him crazy. He had to know we were within the same block as each other, but not the circumstances. I texted back that I had seen her a few minutes ago and that she was fine. The last thing I wanted was for him to panic and, with too little information, make the wrong call.

Pierce climbed aboard his bike and before starting the engine called out something to the other bikers. It looked like he was giving orders. He started the engine and revved the throttle, then pulled out of the lot, turned the corner, and headed east. He made another quick turn and I'd just lost sight of him when I heard the roar of engines behind me. The throttles revved and a few minutes later, the bikes sped out of the lot. I counted at least twenty. It looked like they were all going to follow Pierce until the group split in three at the first intersection and headed in different directions.

"We've got to follow them."

"Easy there, Ranger. There's no more chases. We've got traffic cameras and a hundred cars out there. Relax." He called the number of bikers and the direction they were heading into dispatch and asked for any sightings to be reported. "We got rules now." I sensed he wasn't happy about it, but knew his next job was a security guard.

I was used to taking action myself, not relying on the assets or policies of Miami-Dade. If Susan were wired, we would know their plans, but all we had was the questionable information from the biker sitting next to me. I started to fidget in the seat as Grace finally pulled into traffic. As a federal agent, I wasn't subject to the same rules as the county, and was feeling stifled sitting here doing nothing.

"Where're we going?" I asked, as she turned the corner heading the opposite way from the bikers.

"Got to take lover boy here to lockup. Procedure," Tracy said. "Uniforms'll keep an eye on the bikers."

I needed out of here and now. My gut told me something was about to go down. "Can you drop me at the forensics lab?"

"You going cowboy on us?" he asked.

"Just want to look at things from another angle. The meets have all been in or near the park. I should get back down there." It was all I had and I hoped he bought it. Grace turned and headed toward the lab and I got the impression that they were happy to get rid of me. A few minutes later when they dropped me off, I turned to thank them and gave Tracy a tip of my invisible cowboy hat.

I'd had an idea on the way over. They had their assets and I had mine: Martinez. If there was one thing he was good at besides CCs and BCCs on his emails to make everyone think he had his hands in everything, it was knowing where his people were. I watched Grace pull out of the lot and walked to my truck.

After starting the engine I realized I had nowhere to go. I pressed the phone icon on Martinez's contact page and waited. He answered quickly. "We need to track Susan in real time," I started. I had called rather than text, needing to read his voice to see how he was going to react. Working under pressure was not in his wheelhouse.

He was already watching her. "Got her east on 836. What're they doing, Hunter?"

I could hear the panic in his voice.

"Wait, he's pulled off and stopped."

"Give me the address."

It was his shop. Doubting he'd set up a meet that close to home, I guessed it would be a quick stop. A few minutes later, Martinez confirmed they were moving again.

Before pulling out, I texted Justine. I didn't want her to come out later and see the truck was gone. The phone vibrated before I had a chance to set it down.

"What's going down? I'm hearing about groups of bikers on the scanner."

I briefly explained what had happened.

"You have a plan?"

I wasn't going to say I didn't. "Martinez is tracking Susan's phone. I'm about to follow."

"In your junior ranger truck?"

It wasn't a put down, just the reality. As discreet as the logo and light bar were on the park service truck, Pierce would know it. A minute later, she appeared outside carrying the backpack she used as a purse. I could see the smile on her face and knew I wasn't going alone.

"Pierce is running and he's got Susan."

"Let's go." She started for her car.

I knew there was no talking her out of it and was actually grateful she was coming with me. If I had to choose a partner, she was my first choice. We reached her car and I felt my phone vibrate again. It was Martinez and I put it on speaker.

"Hunter, they're heading north on 95 now. Where the hell are they going?"

I could hear the panic in his voice. Justine started the car and looked at me. I nodded and she pulled out of the lot and headed east toward the Interstate.

Fifteen minutes later, we crossed into Broward County. I was getting out of my comfort zone. I barely knew Miami and had only been this far north once or twice to pick up Allie. Without knowing the area, I looked down at my map app. It made sense that he wanted out of Dade County. If he had been found out, at least that eliminated Miami-Dade from the pursuit. The bikers, however, wouldn't respect that boundary.

I studied the map as Justine drove. The hundred and fifty miles of roads south of Miami ended at Key West. Running north gave him more options. I zoomed out to see where he might be heading and saw the tip of Grand Bahama Island on the right of the screen.

There was the answer, just eighty miles away. With the wind down and the assistance of the Gulfstream's northbound current, it would be an easy ride to Freeport. If you wanted to get to the Bahamas, Port Everglades in Ft. Lauderdale was as good a jump-off point as any. Of course there were extradition treaties, but you could disappear in any one of the hundred small islands there. I wasn't sure if the motorcycle club was more or less of a concern. He hadn't stolen directly from them, but killing a member called for retribution. They would probably hold a grudge for using them as a front, too.

Martinez continued his nervous updates about Susan's position until suddenly her phone stopped moving. Justine continued to Port

Everglades while I zoomed in on Susan's last known position. After connecting the dots in the map app, I was informed it was twenty minutes away. Not very long in South Florida traffic time, but an eternity in real time.

Finally we pulled off 95 and headed east. The location appeared to be a parking lot next to a large marina. Pierce's bike was parked off to the side, and I hopped out of the car to have a look while Justine parked. I was surprised to find the saddlebags unlocked. Reaching around in the empty interior of one, I found Susan's phone. I scanned the area and found no sign of a struggle. Whatever was going on, Susan was still a willing participant.

Twin outboards fired up, directing my attention to the water. It was a false alarm, with only four large fishermen aboard. Turning back to the bike, my eye caught the tire tracks in the gravel. I could see the trail from Pierce's bike; where he had pulled in and then backed up with his feet to park. Off to the side, as if they had come together, were two other pairs of tracks. I didn't need Justine to tell me they were from different bikes. I looked at the marina and then back at the parking lot, trying to figure out where they had gone.

Pierce had proven to be a master at diversion, but my girl was an ace forensics tech. It only took her a few seconds to inspect the tracks and determine that there was more weight on the bikes after stopping here. Pierce had abandoned his bike, making it look like he was taking off by boat, but in actuality, he and Susan were on the road.

There was a whole lot of water out there, but few destinations: the Bahamas, the coastal towns north, or the Keys. You could get lost there, but to the north lay the entire country. Even in the narrow peninsula of Florida there were many more alternatives if they went by land. Leaving Dade County was a smart move. As painful as it was to use their resources, at least I had access to them and Pierce knew it. Just as I was about to ask Justine if she knew anyone in Broward or Palm Beach County, I remembered Stallworth and the Florida Highway Patrol.

Scrolling through my text messages, I found the picture of him and the fish that he had sent the other day. I pressed the phone icon and hoped he was not offshore and out of range while I waited for the call to connect. I thought when it went to voicemail that I would have to make alternate plans, but before I could even update Justine, the phone vibrated.

Apparently Pierce had set up quite a smokescreen. Bikers were well known for sending groups of riders in different directions when pursued. Looked at individually, each bike and rider were often works of art, if you like that kind of thing. As a group, though, they blended together. Stallworth told me there had been radio chatter for the last few hours about several large groups. One was heading west on Alligator Alley, another north on 95, and a third was cruising toward Orlando on the Turnpike. They had all the major routes out of South Florida covered. I had eliminated the first diversion, but now had to narrow it down. At least with the FHP's resources, I might have a chance.

"I'll get back to you in a few," I said, disconnecting the call. Turning to Justine, I explained the situation. Before we could come up with a solution or even a theory, my phone rang again. This time it was Ray. I almost let it go to voicemail, thinking it was some kind of routine park business, but he was not the talkative kind. A three-fingered man could count on one hand how many times Ray had called over the last year.

"Hey," I answered.

"Y'all still lookin' for that crabber we seen the other day?"

I wasn't sure if we were or not, but any information could prove valuable. The boat had already been involved in several incidents. "I'm looking for that FBI agent and Susan. Not sure if she's with him willingly or not." I figured there was no sense holding anything back from him. Another set of eyes at the park could help. "Any chance you can follow it?" I'm up in Broward County on a wild goose chase."

"That damned Susan is more trouble than a gator with the goddamned clap. Sure, got nothing better to do."

I thanked him and turned back to Justine. Our guess that they had gone north could have taken a turn to the south. Pierce had led us fifty miles in the wrong direction.

## 26

I gripped Susan's phone in my hand, hoping it would provide me with a lifeline to her. Despite having talked her into working undercover, I had to remind myself that she had met Pierce, or rather, he had met her, before the murder. Justine and I sat in her car listening to the police scanner app on her phone, wondering what to do next and waiting for an update on the bikers. It was just the standard calls. There had been no reports about the bikers.

"He's not running." I had been replaying the scene when the bikers left the bar and remembered the bags that several, including Pierce, had carried. "And it's not one drop, it's four." The bikers had split into three groups and Pierce had one.

"I bet the others took the straight ammo and Pierce has the drugs," Justine said.

Of course that was it. But that still left us nowhere. "It's not the crabber. He's a motorhead. Six knots an hour would kill him, especially if he thinks we are onto him."

We were missing something and I went back to the bike. The panniers revealed nothing. I opened the seat lid, but there was just the gas tank cap beneath it.

"There's nothing there," Justine said.

I stared at the bike, studying the after-market accessories. There was a custom fairing. It wasn't the typical black plastic addition. The leatherwork was well done and I was running my hands over it, admiring the craftsmanship, when I found a row of small pouches stitched into the bottom.

"Hey." I called Justine over. If there was evidence we needed to handle it properly. She came by my side and gave me a *maybe* look but played along. Returning to the car, she grabbed a baggie with several pairs of gloves, handed me a pair, and put one on herself. We each opened the pouch on our respective sides. Mine had nothing.

"Got something," she said, pulling out a slip of paper.

I wasn't sure what I was expecting, but this was not it. Trying to hide my disappointment, I leaned over her as she unfolded it on the seat. It was a receipt of some kind, and after seeing the store name, I knew what the something we had been missing was. The purchase was for a large quantity of shotshell hulls.

"They have to be loaded and crimped," I said.

"What?"

"There would be a process for loading the shells with the drugs. They would need to be measured, packed, and sealed, requiring special equipment: a grain scale and a reloader." I looked at the store name again. It was a well-known chain.

"Anyone can buy that stuff."

"Anyone can buy it, but you would need something more heavy-duty to do the quantity of shells he's pushing."

"And a gun shop would have that," Justine finished the sentence.

I grabbed my phone from my pocket. Squinting at the thumbnails, I scrolled through the pictures I had taken over the last week. There were several dozen from Alabama Jacks and it took a minute to find the one with the man that had been sitting with Doc. He had the logo with a machine gun. Using my fingers, I zoomed in on the image and saw it was a range in Miami.

"Here it is," I handed the phone to Justine. Pierce had us looking everywhere but Miami, and that's where he had gone. She handed the phone back and I entered the name: Lone Pine Range in the maps app. It was no surprise it was a stone's throw from the biker bar. We ran for the car and started to backtrack south.

"You going to call for backup?" Justine asked as we got onto 595.

The range would certainly be closed now and I wasn't sure what to expect. "Let's have a look first." I didn't think this was going to be as simple as breaking down the doors and arresting him. The evidence I had to this point was circumstantial. I needed something more.

She nodded her acceptance and forty-five minutes later we stopped a few blocks short of the address. It was in a commercial / industrial area with single-story cinderblock buildings. Slowly we approached the address and drove past it twice before spotting the small sign by a solid steel door. There were four bikes and a pickup in front. That would make at least seven people inside, assuming Justine was correct and Pierce and Susan had ridden double.

"There's going to be security cameras for sure at a gun range," Justine said.

With the numbers against us, I didn't have a choice. I called Grace. She said she and Tracy would head over immediately with backup, but it would take about a half-hour.

Justine and I sat down the block, waiting. I glanced at my watch every few minutes, which only increased the tension. After what I guessed was twenty minutes, three men came out of the steel door. The pickup and two bikes took off. That left only Pierce, Susan, and maybe two others. The odds were getting better, and I thought I saw an opportunity when the automatic closer stopped with several inches of daylight showing.

"What are you doing?" Justine grabbed my arm as I opened the door.

"We have to go now. That place will need to be breached if the door closes. I don't expect there's a doorbell."

"What about weapons?"

"It's a gun range, we'll improvise." I used *we* because *wait in the car* were not words she would listen to. This clearly wasn't a public facility and I was counting on all the security being dedicated to keeping people out. She was several feet behind me as I ran across the lot and slid across the building, hoping if there were cameras their focus would be on the direct approaches. It would take a perfectly mounted fisheye lens to cover the long exterior wall.

The door moved just before I reached it, but stopped again as the malfunctioning closer attempted to shut it. I barely got my hand in before I felt the pressure on it as the device attempted to complete its job. We were inside and moved back quickly to the sidewall when the door clicked closed and I heard the distinct sound of an electromagnetic lock engage. We were committed now.

In front of us were several old showcases with different weapons. There was a door behind them with a glass window. The room was dark. To the side were double doors with the same size window, but these were security glass. There were lights on behind them and I guessed they led to the range. For now, we were alone and I approached the closest case. It was open in the back and I pulled out two handguns. While I checked them and ejected the empty magazines, Justine scanned the shelves behind us for bullets. Less than two minutes later, we were armed.

I moved slowly to the double doors and could hear several shots ring out. My immediate reaction was to barge in, but then I remembered where we were. Gun violence might be a problem, but ranges were statistically safe—ridiculously so. In this case, I wasn't so sure and needed to see what was going on beyond the doors. I was just about to go through one of the windows when my phone vibrated. It was Grace and they were outside. I pecked out a quick response for them to be ready, slid my back against the door, and turned my head so I could see inside while presenting as small a profile as possible. Justine was by my side out of view.

Pierce stood with two other men looking at an open case set on a table against the back wall. Susan was in a shooting stance in one of the far stalls. Several shots fired and she turned to reload. I saw her eyes and thought for a second that she had seen me, but she grabbed another magazine, inserted it in the pistol, and resumed firing downrange.

Now that we were here, I wasn't sure what to do. Whatever was in the cases was surely illegal, and Susan was armed. We could burst in and make an arrest, but trying to anticipate what Susan McLeash would do with a loaded weapon was a crapshoot. I was distracted for a second when my phone vibrated. Handing it to Justine, I continued to watch Pierce.

"Grace says there are two men coming in. One is carrying a duffel bag," Justine whispered in my ear.

We were in a bad spot, easily visible to anyone either entering through the front door or leaving the range. I remembered the dark room and ducked under the windows in the door, slid behind the counter, and turned the knob. It opened and just as the entry door opened, Justine and I made it inside and closed the door. We hadn't been seen, but the situation had taken a turn for the worse. Now we were trapped.

Enough light came through the window to dimly light the interior. We were surrounded by workbenches. Rows of tools were neatly lined up on one wall and a large press was on the other. directly across was another door, this one solid. From its location, I guessed that it was a side entrance to the range.

The intermittent firing of Susan's gun was the only sound we could hear. I glanced at Justine, who shrugged her shoulders.

"Should we call in the cavalry?"

I hated to ask for help, but we were in a bind. "Yeah."

She texted Grace and I leaned against the wall, hoping there was something in those cases to justify my actions.

"They're on their way in," Justine whispered. She started typing and a minute later turned back to me. "I gave them the general layout and told them where we were."

I squeezed her thigh, trying to thank her and reassure her at the same time. Her hand met mine and gripped it tightly. We held hands and braced ourselves for whatever was coming next. Then I saw a shadow at the door and the knob turned. Our moment of respite was over.

The only way out was the door to the range and I hoped the element of surprise would work to our advantage. The problem was that Susan had a loaded pistol in her hand, and knowing how trigger happy she was I would somehow have to alert her that it was us.

I released Justine's hand just as the door started to open and nodded to her. Together we went through the solid door. I had no idea if we would be seen or not and couldn't take a chance.

"Susan," I yelled. The barrel of the gun swung in our direction. "Cover Pierce. Miami-Dade is breaching the building now."

She froze, but I had anticipated that. I pointed my pistol at the FBI agent. All I'd really wanted was to have her point it somewhere other than at us. Justine swung her barrel between the group at the table and Susan—just in case.

"Hunter, you idiot, this is a federal investigation."

"Cut it, Pierce. I know you killed the man we found at the lighthouse."

"Stand down now. I'm warning you." He didn't defend himself, but I saw him make a move for something on the table. He came up with a shotgun and I heard the unmistakable sound of the shell enter the chamber. He swung the barrel at Susan.

It was a brilliant tactic. If he'd had a pistol or rifle, he might have been able to get a shot at Justine or me, but there was no clear shot with a shotgun. He'd anticipated my hesitation while I tried to figure out if Susan was with him or against him.

"I had this, Hunter," Susan yelled and set the gun on the counter in front of her.

"Susan and I are just going to walk out of here. I'll release her when I know I'm not being followed."

I could tell from the confused look on her face that she was not happy about being dumped. The sound of steel on steel came from outside, and I expected our reinforcements had arrived. He lowered the weapon, grabbed the bag the men must have brought, and went for Susan. Even in the soundproof range, the shotgun was deafening and I pulled Justine down when I saw Pierce had the barrel pointed at us. Seconds later the sound of the alarm blared as he crashed through the emergency exit door. My ears were ringing so I didn't hear Justine scream.

She was down and blood was pouring from her leg. Several darts from the flechette had found her. Looking around, I heard a shot and ducked. The two men left behind were back to back, one firing at us, the other at the two figures dressed in black with bulletproof vests that had just crashed through the door.

Our help might have arrived, but we were in the line of fire. Grabbing Justine, I pulled her back through the side door. With one hand on my pistol and the other with a firm grasp on her arm, we entered the next room, surprising the two men at the workbench. One was weighing and packing the shells; the other was using the large press to crimp them. Weapons being discharged in a firing range was standard procedure, so they'd had no idea what was going on. They froze and I took a chance. "Help her. Get some pressure on the wound and I'll keep you out of this."

There was no hesitation on their part and I touched Justine's cheek before heading back through the door to the shop. "Call an ambulance," I yelled at Grace and headed out the front door.

Pierce had made it to one of the bikes and was heading out of the parking lot. There were several options open to me and I took the one my anger-fueled brain chose. It wasn't to follow or call in his location. I raised my arm, aimed for the rear wheel, and fired two shots. He turned the corner and I turned away, thinking I had missed.

A few seconds later, I heard a skid and a crash.

## 27

"So, what do you want to do?" I asked Allie.

"I can't believe you're asking that."

I might have been smart enough to put a crooked FBI agent behind bars, but dealing with a fifteen-year-old was a different matter altogether. I had found that one of the techniques I used to interview people worked on her as well, and just stayed quiet. It was an uncomfortable minute. It was kind of like playing chicken, and I was about to say something and admit defeat when she broke the silence.

"See Justine, duh."

Another proud dad moment. "Of course," I said, and put the truck in reverse. Jane had waited until we left and she backed out behind me. I breathed in relief when she turned left after we made a right out of the parking lot.

"You gonna let me drive one of these days?"

Allie had been proud to inform me she had just gotten her learner's permit. It was one of those things I'd missed as a weekend parent. "Sure. How about we give it a try down in Homestead later?"

"That'd be cool." She put her head down and started typing into her phone. I remembered Justine thinking she had a boyfriend and I was trying to get up the nerve to ask. Usually we made plans for our next visit whenever we were together, but now, with Justine in the hospital, we were quiet.

We reached Jackson Memorial and found Sid by her side. Justine was awake, and Allie went right to her. I stood back, trying to fight the tears, watching the two people I cared most about.

"They say she should be out in a few days," Sid said, breaking the silence. "Doctors around here seem awful young, but I'm watching them." He turned and squeezed Justine's hand, kissed her on the forehead, and turned to the door. "Got to go keep an eye on Vance, too," he said, shaking his head, and muttering something about the incompetence of today's youth, walked out.

I took his place beside Justine and kissed her. Her eyes were watering and I couldn't tell if it was from pain or happiness. "You okay?" I asked.

"You go check the tide tables for day after tomorrow. We're going fishing. Diving might have to wait a bit."

This was the first time she was conscious enough to hear what had happened and I recounted the story for her and Allie. I could see the mix of admiration and fear in Allie's eyes as I told her about Justine getting shot and the takedown of Pierce.

"What happened to him?" she asked.

"The FBI is going to prosecute him for the murder and drugs. He'll get what he deserves."

"And what about Susan?" Justine asked.

"She came out of it looking pretty good. Probably get a commendation for her undercover work. I have a feeling she'll be officially reinstated now."

"And the saga continues," Justine said.

I just nodded. Allie and I stayed until Justine fell asleep, and then we quietly left the room.

"So, are you going to ask her to marry you or what?" Allie asked when we were in the hallway.

And I had been worried about asking her if she had a boyfriend.

Get the next book in the Kurt Hunter Mystery Series
**How many lives is a cover-up worth**

When a bridge collapses and kills six people, National Park Service Special Agent Kurt Hunter is drawn into an tangled web of finger pointing and political machinations. With the bridge debris scheduled to be turned into an artificial reef in the park, Kurt and Justine are in a race against time to find the party responsible.

But things are not as simple as they appear and soon powerful political figures turn the case into a power struggle to save one of the countries biggest universities.

**Get it now!**

**Thanks For Reading**

If you liked the book please leave a review here

For more information please check out my web page:
https://stevenbeckerauthor.com/

Or follow me on Facebook:
https://www.facebook.com/stevenbecker.books/

I'm also on Instagram as: stevenbeckerauthor

**Get my starter library First Bite for Free!
when you sign up for my newsletter**

http://eepurl.com/-obDj

First Bite contains the first book in each of Steven Becker's series:

- **Wood's Reef**
- **Pirate**
- **Bonefish Blues**

*By joining you will receive one or two emails a month about what I'm doing and special offers.*

*Your contact information and privacy are important to me. I will not spam or share your email with anyone.*

**Wood's Reef**
"A riveting tale of intrigue and terrorism, Key West characters in their

*full glory! Fast paced and continually changing direction Mr Becker has me hooked on his skillful and adventurous tales from the Conch Republic!"*

**Pirate**
*"A gripping tale of pirate adventure off the coast of 19th Century Florida!"*

**Bonefish Blues**"*I just couldn't put this book down. A great plot filled with action. Steven Becker brings each character to life, allowing the reader to become immersed in the plot."*

**Get them now (http://eepurl.com/-obDj)**

**Also By Steven Becker**

**Kurt Hunter Mysteries**

*Backwater Bay*

*Backwater Channel*

*Backwater Cove*

*Backwater Key*

*Backwater Pass (July 2018)*

**Mac Travis Adventures**

*Wood's Relic*

*Wood's Reef*

*Wood's Wall*

*Wood's Wreck*

*Wood's Harbor*

*Wood's Reach*

*Wood's Revenge*

*Wood's Betrayal*

**Tides of Fortune**

*Pirate*

*The Wreck of the Ten Sail*

*Haitian Gold*

**Will Service Adventure Thrillers**

*Bonefish Blues*

*Tuna Tango*

*Dorado Duet*

**Storm Series**

*Storm Rising*

*Storm Force*

Made in the USA
Las Vegas, NV
13 November 2023